THE STRIKE ZON

SLAM was on a fast train. Positioning themselves back-to-back, Slater and Hawke got set to clean house.

Whipsawing 7.62 mm rivets flailed from the wailing MG at Slater's hip, chopping down the charging point mercs who were heaving steel on a flat-out run.

Hawke's own hardware bucked in his fists, too. Glowing tracer rounds zigzagged through the night as the Ultimax 100 LMG cycled out its annihilating fire stream.

The combined effect of the two jackhammering auto-weapons was pure, bloody mayhem.

Their bodies jerking and shuddering as they became grotesquely animated under a pounding wave front of high velocity body manglers, La Carne's mercs flung their arms into the air, firing autobursts at the moon, then dropped down to the dirt.

Before long, Slater and Hawke's fire storm had punched out an escape corridor for the two SLAM commandos.

DAN MATTHEWS

SLAM

Force Option

A GOLD EAGLE BOOK FROM
WORLDWIDE®

TORONTO • NEW YORK • LONDON
AMSTERDAM • PARIS • SYDNEY • HAMBURG
STOCKHOLM • ATHENS • TOKYO • MILAN
MADRID • WARSAW • BUDAPEST • AUCKLAND

First edition April 1993

ISBN 0-373-63407-2

Special thanks and acknowledgment to David Alexander for his contribution to this work.

FORCE OPTION

Printed in U.S.A.

"Bomb Medellín and the war on drugs is over."
—FBI agent

"First we are going to cut it off. Then we are going to kill it."
—General Colin Powell, speaking of the Iraqi army

PROLOGUE

The crazy American sat all alone drinking wine at a table in the dockside bar. The cantina was otherwise empty. It wasn't yet siesta time, and most of the bars were still closed.

The proprietor had opened up early because of the exceptionally hot weather but also because he knew that his customer would be coming around as usual.

The cantina wasn't located in a good section of the city. It wasn't a place where it was advisable for an American to be found alone, not if he valued his life. Yet this man walked the streets of the Barcelona waterfront without fear and in recent weeks had become a regular patron.

On the street outside, automobile horns blared and the shouts and laughter of passersby drifted into the bar, muted by the gathering heat of early afternoon. The American reached out and poured himself a final glass of the dark red house wine, emptying the bottle.

Soon the glass, too, was drained. As he slapped it down on the tabletop, three hard-looking men swaggered into the cantina.

The leader of the pack strode up to the bar and spoke a few words to the old man standing behind it, who was wiping glasses with a dirty rag. The proprietor stared wide-eyed at the big, mean-looking American and nodded to the newcomer. A moment later he disappeared through a doorway behind the bar.

That left the American alone with the three hardmen.

The trio strode confidently toward his table, their eyes boring into him insolently. The two on the flanks broke right and left and took up positions at either side of his chair. The leader assumed a belligerent stance directly in front of the table and sneered down at the lone American.

The hardman had straight black hair combed back over his skull and held in place with a sweatband. His brown eyes were flat and menacing, set in a blocky face. He was more muscular than his companions, with massive shoulders and a barrel chest.

He threw a challenging glance at the seated man and spit on the tabletop. Quickly pulling a hunting knife from a sheath at his belt, he leaned forward and brandished it threateningly.

"You stinking maggot," he snarled. "You know what I do with this knife? I cut off your—"

A .357 Magnum round crashed through the heavy oak tabletop and shattered the bladesman's face as though it were made of bric-a-brac. His lower jaw vanished in a spurt of crimson, and brain matter gushed from the exit wound at the back of his skull.

As he sagged to the floor, the other two men were already whipping hardware from holsters concealed beneath their loose-cut, gaudily patterned shirts.

But by then the American was on his feet. Ducking sideways, he bowled over the pistol packer to his right as he turned to sight on the other gunman and pumped two quick rounds into the center of his chest, propelling him backward and sending him crashing into the wall.

Recovering his wits, the thug on the floor fisted his .38-caliber Colt and began snapping off rounds in blind rage and panic. The big American tucked, rolled and dived, darting for cover behind chairs, tables and the thick wood beams supporting the cantina's roof, then sprang back out into the open to stand smiling at the antagonist whose revolver was now pointing at his face.

The gunman was breathing hard. His suspicious eyes darted left and right. What was going down here, anyway? he wondered. Did the crazy American want to die? Whether he did or not, the hardman decided to send him to hell and dropped the hammer on the Colt's firing pin.

Click.

Click.

Click.

"You should have counted, *compadre,*" the American growled, reaching around his back to ease the silver-plated .357 Magnum revolver from the holster beneath his wide-cut tank top. "Rule number one—always check your ammo supply."

Frozen in place, the outmaneuvered hitter watched as the American flipped open the Magnum's cylinder and emptied six brass casings onto the floor.

"You know what the second rule is, *compadre?*" the American asked as he coolly began thumbing fresh cartridges into their slots.

The Spaniard didn't respond. He had been too busy fumbling for a speed loader in his hip pocket and had already managed to eject the spent casings and slam the live rounds into the wheel gun. In another second he would be ready to shoot.

With a flick of his wrist he clicked the lethal cylinder back into place and whipped his heat into play.

The big American fired a pulse beat sooner.

The single hollownose punched through the Spaniard's chest, shearing through vital organs and inflicting massive physical trauma. The dying man grunted as his arms flew up and his legs buckled beneath him, then he sagged to the sawdust-covered planking of the cantina floor.

"The second rule is *never fuck with me,*" the American rasped as he pumped two more dum-dums into the jerking, twitching figure at his feet.

Just then the American heard the sound of footfalls from the cantina's entrance. He spun around to see the newcomer framed in the open doorway, silhouetted against the glaring light that poured in from the sun-baked street.

The man in the doorway put his hands up.

"That was very good, Mr. Slater," he said in thickly accented English. "An ample demonstration of your abilities. May I enter?"

Slater gestured to one side with the gun barrel. The newcomer strode in confidently. He was a middle-aged man with close-cropped gray hair, hatless and tieless in a white tropical suit, once powerfully built, though now gone to seed.

To the practiced eye, he had *merc* written all over him. The American knew the man. His name was Karl Spengler, and he was a Belgian national who'd started off with Project Phoenix in Indochina and now earned his keep as a middleman and international deal maker. Sometimes it was arms, other times it was personnel, and still other times it was intelligence.

"Hands in front of you," the American growled. "Palms down on the table."

Spengler did as ordered. Stepping over the bodies of the three terminated hitters, the American seated himself across from him with his back to the wall, the chair back in front of him.

"These three were throwaways," Spengler admitted. "A test to see if Deal Slater is the man he once was."

"Did I pass?"

"Flying colors, Mr. Slater." Spengler lit a thin cheroot that he had slid from his shirt pocket. "I have a proposition for you."

"Who says I want to hear it?"

"I'll be frank," answered Spengler. "Following events in the Iraqi desert, you were dishonorably discharged from Delta. The unfortunate circumstances are widely known in certain circles. Denied a military pension, you became an expatriate. You've been drifting for months, Mr. Slater. You are down to your last nickel. I apologize if I appear insensitive, but facts, after all, are facts."

Slater relaxed his grip on the .357.

"What's your pitch?" he asked, laying the wheel gun flat on the tabletop.

PART ONE:
THE SHEEP DIP

1

Deal Slater rode in the back seat of a chauffeured, air-conditioned BMW across the blacktop highway and up into the wrinkled gray-brown hills of Guadalajara. He was on his way to a sit-down with the man for whom the Belgian was acting as a talent scout.

Slater had cleaned up his act. The Cardin suit he wore was new, the lenses of his designer sunglasses squeaky clean. He had even taken a bath in honor of the occasion—something Slater hadn't bothered doing frequently of late.

The merc free-lancer had been informed that the man who had sent the Belgian ran a no-nonsense operation. He didn't do business with freaks, weirdos and airheads. He was a heavyweight and didn't tolerate lightweights. Bullshit walked. Slater had to dress to impress.

Slater folded his arms across his chest and stared at the backs of the two heads in front of him. The giant sitting behind the wheel of the black luxury sedan had identified himself as Montana and said he was a native Venezuelan.

In Spanish his handle translated as "Mountain," Slater knew. The tag fit the guy to a tee. Montana was big all over, with outsize, muscular hands and a large fleshy head perched on a thickset neck.

The other enforcer type who sat up front next to Montana was called Delgado, or "Slim." Unlike Montana, Delgado was of medium height and build and was also a flashy dresser. His tailored shirt was unbuttoned to the navel. A ton of gold chains hung from his neck, and at least a couple of pounds were carried on his fingers in the form of massive rings.

Slater didn't like his two playmates at all. He didn't even like their nicknames. He had a feeling he wasn't going to like too damn much about what lay in store, except maybe the satisfaction of putting his talents to profitable use again.

Soon Slater could see his destination looming up ahead on the right as Montana swung the BMW onto a turnoff lane. It was an estate perched high atop one of the hills rising back from the coastal plain.

Although it had been designed by some trendy California architect in the postmodern style with eight walls of chrome and glass, the place reminded Slater of nothing so much as a fortress. He knew that's exactly what it was. The house was called the Octagon, and it belonged to a druglord named Francisco Terra Nova.

MASON HAWKE SWIVELED around in his chair to face Eddie Bishop. Hawke was young, but no shavetail. He'd paid his blood dues in covert firezones stretching from Afghanistan to Iraq. He had close-cropped blond hair, which made him look younger than his actual years, and a lightweight commo set was fitted around the top of his head.

Some people liked to joke that Hawke had been born with a computer chip in place of a soul. Hawke was a whiz where anything electronic was concerned and knew more about the esoterica of techno-military jargon than most of the techs themselves. He was also an expert lockpick.

Bishop was shorter than Hawke but broader around the shoulders and chest. He had the stature, build and looks of the middleweight boxer he had been at West Point.

He was also older than Hawke by a couple of years. Bishop's specialties were weapons, sharpshooting and demolition. His marksmanship had earned him medals, though they were covert medals that could never be publicly worn.

Bishop was carefully cleaning the parts of a takendown Uzi SMG. He'd cleaned the weapon before but believed that even a single particle of dust in the wrong place could mean disaster. Guns frequently jammed and they always picked the wrong times to do so.

"What's going down?" Bishop asked as he looked up from the metal parts scattered on the table in front of him.

Hawke had just reacted to a beep-tone from his equipment and was keying in a command sequence at the keyboard of one of the computer consoles.

"Keyhole just moved into position. Weather conditions are good. I'm starting to receive telemetry."

"Great, especially if cloud patterns hold," Bishop acknowledged, fitting the sear together with other components making up the trigger-housing assembly of the Uzi. "Let me have a look."

Bishop sidled over and examined the high-resolution image on the large console screen. The real-time video telemetry was originating from one hundred fifty miles up in space.

A Keyhole, or KH-11 Intelsat—able to detect and track objects as small as six inches—was beaming images of the car carrying Deal Slater toward his destination. The car was clearly visible as it climbed the twisting road into the mountains.

The van in which Hawke and Bishop sat was outfitted with the cutting edge in sophisticated computer and telemetry equipment. Operations time on the KH-11 had been specially secured from the National Security Agency by executive order.

The President had personally scissored through the bureaucratic red tape and sanctioned an operation buried so deeply that only the CinC and one other man not in the field knew about it. This was the team's White House and Pentagon liaison man, Jack Callixto, who was based stateside in D.C.

Deal Slater was the point in Operation Southern Star, the first mission of a newly sanctioned offensive against the gigantic narcotic cartels that in some cases had subverted entire governments.

Agencies like DEA and the defunct Centac, which could only prosecute druglords, had bobbled all the plays so far.

Buy-bust stings and elaborate paper chases leading to the occasional prosecution of a major-league player in the narcotrafficking arena had left too many loose ends untied and created more problems than they had solved.

Direct action was needed desperately, needed now.

Action in the form of an elite commando unit known as SLAM. Search Locate Annihilate Missions were the detail's presidentially mandated role.

SLAM was a three-man strike team, operating below the threshold of the opposition's security network. Each elite shadow warrior was handpicked by

Deal Slater, and together they would act as the Davids who would take down the Goliaths of the world's major criminal enterprises.

"Slater's getting out of the car," Hawke reported to Bishop, and pointed out the diminutive shape on the glowing screen.

"Okay," Bishop put in, snapping a clip of parabellums into the receiver of the freshly oiled and polished Uzi. "That means it's show time."

2

The room's decor was a mixture of sterile modernism and gaudy bad taste. It was filled with hangers-on and people with business to transact. The ostentation was just as excessive as the ego of the man who owned the house.

Even in the world of major-league narcotraffickers, Francisco Terra Nova stood in a class by himself. Terra Nova was good at what he did, so good that nobody could touch him. Not the Mexican feds, not the American DEA—nobody. It was said that his influence extended not only into the upper echelons of the Mexican government, but into the power centers of the U.S., Canada and Europe, as well.

Unlike his Colombian partner and ally, Rogelio la Carne—the scion of landed gentry who claimed they could trace their ancestry all the way back to the original Spanish colonists—Terra Nova had begun his criminal career with nothing except street smarts and a willingness to exploit any opportunity for gain in his lifelong quest for power.

Despite the differences in their backgrounds, it was this unquenchable thirst for power that drove both of them on and had made them natural allies. It was power more than the immense revenues derived from drug trafficking that was the object of both men. Drugs were only a means to gain that ultimate end.

That's what made the Mexico-Colombia axis forged between Terra Nova and la Carne so potentially dangerous and ranked the criminal enterprise as SLAM's priority-one target. It definitely warranted Slater's conducting a hazardous dangle operation in the heart of Terra Nova's power base.

There was much more at stake than merely the thousands of tons of grass and coke that was being funneled into the States through Mexican corridors each year.

The potentially greater threat involved the nascent power alliance established between the two men and what it portended for global security.

With their East German, Soviet and Middle Eastern patrons either out of the business of financing insurrectionist warfare or having drastically cut back their clandestine aid, international terrorists were now desperate for funding.

The former East German Stasi, the Romanian Securitate and the dreaded Czech secret police, among others, had all established "rat lines" for escaping personnel that led where the original Nazi rat lines had once gone: to Mexico and South and Central America.

These elements of former secret police and intelligence bureaucracies possessed money, know-how and international connections. Terra Nova and Carne were natural choices as surrogates for projecting that power in the form of new and more violent offensives by reorganized terrorist cells into America and Western Europe.

This factor was what made SLAM anxious to smash the cartel and put both Terra Nova and Carne out of commission.

Sipping a drink, Slater waited for Terra Nova's arrival as he looked out the room's big picture window. He had a breathtaking view of half of northern Mexico laid out before him, with the Pacific sparkling to the west.

Soon Slater turned and saw Terra Nova walking into the room with a striking-looking blonde on his arm.

The druglord was wearing a cashmere sport coat and color-coordinated charcoal pants. His black hair was tied back in a small knot at the back of his head, and a gold stud glittered in his right earlobe. His movements were languid, those of a man used to commanding attention from everyone around him.

The blonde was slim but full breasted. The clingy black satin ensemble she wore did more to advertise than conceal her assets. Enough gold to bankrupt a Third World country glittered at her throat, fingers and wrists.

Instantly the buzz of conversation diminished. The blonde whispered something into Terra Nova's ear, and they both laughed.

Slater experienced the sense of charisma coming from the drug baron right away. It was something in the eyes and the strutting walk. Hitler had it. Mussolini had it. Terra Nova had it, too—the power to make people do as he wished them to by the mere force of his personality.

"I'm glad to meet you, Mr. Slater," the druglord said in a cultivated voice with only a hint of a Mexican accent. "But my friend Venice says you have 'cop's eyes.'" A gleam Slater didn't like came into Terra Nova's own piercing eyes. "You aren't a cop, are you?"

"I think Venice has an overactive imagination," Slater said.

"Possibly," replied Terra Nova with a smile. "She has many overactive things. But come into my private office. We can talk better there."

With a pat on the rump he sent the blonde scurrying away, though not without a backward glance at Slater, which might have meant anything at all.

Slater followed Terra Nova into a side room and down a short corridor hung with Impressionist oil paintings. The plush carpeted office was spacious but lacking windows, a sign that its walls were copper clad and bug proof.

The trappings of power filled it. Bookcases containing expensive volumes lined the walls, and a large globe stood on a polished wooden stand. A huge desk of gleaming oak dominated the room. Above it was a bank of security screens linked to external cameras, and behind it a high wing chair of soft Italian kidskin.

On top of the desk Slater recognized classified CIA and Joint Special Operations Command documents. They were UMBRA and NOFORN coded, meaning the secrecy clearances normally required to read them were the highest possible.

Terra Nova smiled.

"Yes, I know all about you, Mr. Slater," he said, leaning back in his chair. "As you can see, I have friends in high places. What they inform me is that you are a wronged man, a man who was betrayed by his country and cast out into the cold."

Slater stayed silent, watching Terra Nova through hooded eyes and letting him play out his string.

"You see that I'm well acquainted with you," Terra Nova went on in perfect idiomatic American English. "Now let me tell you why you're here. I need a guy with the abilities you have to do a very important job for me. A job for which you will of course be handsomely compensated.''

Terra Nova reached into the pocket of his cashmere sport coat and pulled out a wad of U.S. currency. He flipped the flash roll across the desk at Slater.

''There's five thousand dollars, just for listening to my offer,'' he told Slater. ''You decide whether you want to accept it or not. If you don't, that's okay. You can still walk.''

Slater reached across the desk and picked up the wad of cash. He riffled through the hunk of money. The bills looked crisp enough to make a tossed salad. Slater flipped the roll back onto the top of the desk.

''What's your pitch?'' he asked.

Terra Nova grinned. He knew that sitting before him was a man he could do business with.

''I would like somebody removed from the population count,'' he calmly told Slater. ''I don't care how you do it, but I need it done fast.''

''I'm still interested,'' Slater returned.

''Good,'' Terra Nova said.

He produced a manila file folder from a drawer. Walking around the front of the desk, he handed the dossier to Slater. There were a couple of six-by-seven black-and-white glossies in the folder of a heavyset guy with strong Hispanic features. From their graininess and the distortion of the image, they were obviously surveillance photos shot with a long-range telephoto lens.

"His name is Rudy Gomez," Terra Nova told Slater. "He has been given immunity by your government in the Federal Witness Protection Program. Next week he will testify before a specially convened grand jury. Needless to say, his testimony would be highly undesirable to my organization."

Slater closed the file folder and laid it atop the polished surface of the desk.

"What did he do," Slater asked, "leave the cap off the toothpaste tube one too many times?"

"What went down between Gomez and myself is my business," Terra Nova told Slater without smiling. "The only thing I want to know is if you're in or out. And I'm afraid I need to know right now."

Slater had no doubt that if he gave the wrong answer to Terra Nova he'd wind up floating facedown in the Gulf of Mexico. What the druglord wanted was known south of the border as *una muerte de prueba,* a test killing. It was a common way of checking out an executioner's abilities.

"You just bought yourself the best," Slater said as he slipped the wad of money into his pocket.

3

The sun had risen to its zenith, and Slater instantly felt the ovenlike heat sear his face as he exited the air-conditioned BMW.

Montana was Slater's traveling companion again, though Delgado wasn't along for the trip to the airport. The Venezuelan spoke rarely, which suited Slater just fine.

Montana was to facilitate Slater's transfer onto a Pan Am jet bound for Colorado, where the smuggler whom Terra Nova had hired him to whack had been relocated by the Feds.

Unknown to Montana, the BMW he was steering through the Mexican hills was being tracked via KH-11 satellite down-link from the surveillance van parked on a Guadalajara side street where Hawke and Bishop were following the sedan's every move.

Conducting surveillance by the roundabout method of peering down at SLAM's leader through a camera lens hanging in outer space was necessary because Terra

Nova maintained complete control over everything that went down in his immediate environment.

Every room in the Octagon was bugged and all vehicles regularly swept for concealed surveillance devices by a competent staff. There was no way that Slater could carry any signaling gear on his person.

James Bond type gadgets had their place in the operations zone, but the burst-transmitter concealed as a calculator or pocket computer wouldn't mesh well with Slater's "legend" as an expatriate American mercenary—a hard, embittered and violent man who would not normally be carrying around expensive consumer electronics.

Eventually such items would be taken from him and given a thorough checkout. Terra Nova was no fool. Even if he couldn't discern the dual function of covert spy gear, their mere presence on a guy like Slater would be a red flag—and ultimately a death warrant.

Only by conducting their signals and communications Intelligence on passive and subtechnological levels could Hawke and Bishop keep tabs on Slater's progress. But the major drawback of this approach was that it didn't provide for a method by which they could efficiently employ two-way communication.

There was no option for Hawke and Bishop to inform Slater that Gomez had turned jackrabbit and taken off from the single-story ranch house in Colorado where the Feds had been keeping him on ice.

Gomez had been flipped by the Feds and had laid the groundwork for the Terra Nova dangle and infiltration op. The ex-member of Terra Nova's inner circle had enough inside dirt to put his former boss away for a major stretch in the slammer.

The smuggler knew that Terra Nova wanted him dead and believed his only chance at staying alive lay in dropping a dime on the Mexican kingpin. That meant cooperating with the American Justice Department and testifying before a grand jury. Gomez was the perfect bait to lure a big fish like Terra Nova into a fatal sting setup.

With Slater turned from Delta commando to merc-for-hire and the word put out that his services were available for the right price, conditions were optimized for a get-together between himself and Terra Nova. After all, Terra Nova only messed with the best and Slater was the cream of the crop. Slater's arrival on the free-lance scene was another kind of bait dangled in front of the drug honcho. One he had bitten hook, line and sinker.

A CANVAS LUGGAGE BAG stuffed with clean shirts, a new toothbrush and an old shaving kit slung over his shoulder, Slater walked into the terminal at Guadalajara International. Like all Third World airport terminals, it was hot, crowded and watched over by strutting cops in paramilitary uniforms who looked more eager to bust heads than to help perplexed flyers find their departure gates.

Slater checked himself in at the airline ticket counter and confirmed his booking for the next flight out to Colorado, scheduled to depart in twenty minutes.

While Slater was walking, tickets in hand, toward the plane's departure gate, Hawke, in mirrored sunglasses, went into the men's room in the main terminal area and crossed toward the third stall in from the rear wall.

The stall was a prearranged dead drop for messages.

Hawke had downed an ice-cold bottle of Carta Blanca at an airport lounge, so there would be no problem about producing a realistic-sounding tinkle for the benefit of any listeners.

The toilet was the old-fashioned kind still found in public rest-room areas outside the U.S., complete with an overhead septic tank and a pull chain. Hawke tugged the chain and quickly reached up to slap the yellow sticky pad onto the top of the tank where it was invisible to view from below.

Having executed the message drop, Hawke sauntered out of the men's room and took a circuitous path through the terminal that was designed to shake off any surveillance.

When he was certain that nobody was shadowing him, Hawke grabbed a green taxicab into the city and got off several blocks from where the surveillance van with Bishop was located in the parking lot of a time-share condo catering to rich gringos.

The van sported Texas plates, and it was neither too beat-up looking nor too spanking new to attract attention. Cruising from one car park to another, Hawke and Bishop were able to remain in territory where *norteamericanos* and American-style vehicles wouldn't attract an inordinate amount of attention from the locals.

"Did you make the drop?" Bishop asked as Hawke entered the surveillance vehicle.

"Count on it," Hawke replied.

SLATER CHECKED his watch and pushed through a swinging door marked *Caballeros,* smiling at the fact that it often wasn't a "men's" room south of the border but a "gentlemen's" room. One more endearing trait of America's southern neighbors, who were always gentlemanly when taking a leak. He saw that the drop stall was unoccupied and walked into it, bolting the door behind him.

Standing over the stall, he went through the motions, then checked for a drop message while the noise of the flushing toilet covered the sounds of his movements. He felt the sticky pad jammed up near the wall atop the overhead tank.

A quick scan of the message pad told Slater that he was now faced with a serious problem: Gomez had taken a powder on the Feds. He crumpled the small paper square and chucked it into the whirling vortex at the center of the commode.

With the panicked smuggler loose-cannoning around, the operation had lost the crucial linchpin that tied everything together. No Gomez, no *muerte de prueba.* No *muerte de prueba,* no infiltration of the Terra Nova organization. No infiltration of the organization, the op turned sour fast. All the preparation, all the hard work, would come to nothing.

Slater would have to go through the motions of tracking Gomez down and see what happened. But he realized that if Hawke and Bishop didn't get to the scared drug-runner first and persuade him to cooperate, then Slater might just have to smoke him for real.

4

The phone rang in the hotel room. Slater picked it up on the second ring.

"Yeah?"

"Change of plans, *señor*," the caller said, and Slater recognized Terra Nova's richly timbered voice. "Our friend has skipped town."

"Tell me about it," Slater answered with a snort of laughter. "I been all over the place. No offense, but your Intel leaves a lot to be desired."

"You're not the only one who's pissed," Terra Nova agreed. "Give me a callback in five minutes. I've got some new information I want you to have."

The line cut off.

Slater went to the closet and unzipped a blue nylon luggage bag. Wrapped in bubble pack inside was a Cryptacec 242 portable telephone line encryption-decryption unit.

One thing about Terra Nova: he didn't mess around. Everything about him was state of the art.

The Mexican had handed Slater the ten-thousand-dollar unit and told him to use it when communicating with him. Terra Nova wasn't into his people or himself pumping quarters into pay telephones. That was the mark of second-raters, and second-raters didn't last long in the fast lane.

Slater plugged the full-duplex signal-hopping transmitter into the phone unit's modular jack and dialed one of the numbers with a Mexican area code that Terra Nova had given him on the keypad mounted on the front of the compact unit.

The encryption-decryption was completely transparent and compatible with all existing phone lines. Electronic handshaking protocols automatically set the communications parameters.

"Slater," Terra Nova said smoothly as the phone was picked up on the first ring. "You're following procedure?"

"You'd know if I weren't," Slater growled in reply. The Cryptacec's LED panel would show if an incoming call had been placed on an open line, he knew damn well. Terra Nova was testing him out in the smarts department.

"Just checking," Terra Nova apologized. "You already know that Gomez bolted on the Feds. I know where he ran to. The little cockroach was spotted in the Bronx a few hours ago. Book yourself on the next flight to New York. Keep in touch in the usual manner.''

The phone line abruptly went dead. Terra Nova was careful about what he said on any phone, secure or not, delivering orders in excellent English that could be interpreted one way or the other. He was a dude who left no smoking guns.

Slater stashed the Cryptacec unit back in his luggage. Hooking the hotel room phone back up to its modular wall jack, he rang up the front desk and told the girl he was checking out.

"Any problem, sir?" the concerned female voice asked with a Southwestern twang.

"Nothing you probably couldn't fix, honey," Slater retorted.

"How do you mean, sir?" the girl asked, her voice slightly changing pitch.

"Use your imagination," he told her. "You'll figure it out."

Terra Nova had eyes and ears everywhere, and Slater had to stay in character. The role he was playing was that of a Special Forces renegade carrying a king-size chip on his shoulder. He had to talk and behave like such a man at all times or Terra Nova would smoke him out and then smoke him permanently.

There was the sound of the receiver being handed over to somebody, and an angry male voice soon came on the line.

"Is there any problem, *sir?*" the deeper voice asked in a tone of challenge. Clearly people in Englewood, Colorado, were not blasé about customers making passes at young female staffers.

Slater hung up on the speaker, then called the airport. The soonest available flight out wasn't till that night, he learned. Slater booked the flight over the phone, charging it to his credit card.

Then he showered, dressed and headed downstairs. The scowling hotel manager at the front desk was glaring daggers at him as Slater checked out of the hotel then went into the bar in the lobby. He had a couple of hours to kill yet.

Slater hoped that was all he'd have to kill. Blowing away a bad guy in the heat of action or the cold-blooded pursuit of justified means was no problem.

In fact, that's just what was waiting for Terra Nova and his Colombian associate, Rogelio la Carne. When the time came, Slater would drop the hammer on both dope barons with equal pleasure.

But Gomez was another matter. The guy was basically a low-level smurf who'd gotten in way over his head and had lost his nerve when push finally came to shove.

Icing him wouldn't be an act of justice, Slater knew. It would be a stone-cold execution.

5

The battle-scarred blue '79 TransAm had seen better days. It had been painted and patched too many times in too many places. But there were 427 horses under the hood, a Cyclone exhaust system, a Hurst Pro-Matic four-on-the-floor and a custom-installed Hays clutch.

The TransAm could blow the doors off any other vehicle on the street.

Wearing denim jackets over hooded sweats and caps with the elastic bands turned frontward homeboy-style, Hawke and Bishop sat watching the apartment building in the South Bronx they had traced Gomez to.

The apartment belonged to his sister Wilhelmina, who was out of town for the next few weeks visiting relatives in San Juan, Puerto Rico. Gomez was keeping a low profile, venturing twice a day from the apartment to buy some groceries, beers and smokes.

Otherwise he was lying low, doing a couch-potato routine in front of the TV.

The two SLAM personnel had been scoping out the building for the past two days. Now that they had

Gomez's pattern of activity down, it was time to bust Gomez and rub his nose in some of the mess he'd made of this neatly planned operation.

"THERE GOES OUR MAN," Hawke said from the TransAm's passenger side.

Bishop squinted into the rearview and saw the stocky, goateed Hispanic exit the front doors of the apartment building. Gomez then stood on the top step puffing on a cigarette. He looked left and then he looked right. He hung around until two loud-talking, arm-swinging homeboys sauntered on past.

"Paranoid dude," Bishop remarked.

"But one who definitely has something to feel paranoid about," returned Hawke as he continued to scope out Gomez.

Satisfied that the coast was clear, Gomez hit the sidewalk on his way to the bodega around the corner for his regular junk food and beer pit stop.

When Gomez had turned the corner, Hawke climbed out of the car and hustled into the building vestibule. Hawke picked the lobby door's lock in under two minutes, using a rake pick and tension wrench to stroke the pin tumblers of its keyway into lineup position, then snap the lock. Twenty years ago he could simply have rung a bell to gain admittance. Not anymore. The times had changed.

From the lobby, Hawke took the creaking, graffiti-emblazoned elevator car up to the fifth floor apartment.

The locks on Gomez's door would be a little harder than the lobby entrance. The primary difficulty was that there were three of them, all quality items with armored security plates, and on top of that Hawke had to pick the locks in the limited time frame without leaving any telltale marks behind to alert the skittish Gomez. Hawke estimated the job would take him fifteen minutes. At least, he hoped it would.

Taking the Walkabout earbuds from around his neck and putting them over his ears, Hawke activated the compact transceiver clipped to his belt, which was specially camouflaged to resemble an AM-FM Walkabout.

The unit was tuned to the frequency of the identical transceiver carried by Bishop, who was acting as spotter in the TransAm. If any hitches came up, Bishop would be able to alert Hawke in plenty of time.

Hawke used a lifter pick and tension wrench on the first, then the second lock. He was halfway through the third lock when he heard Bishop's voice in his ear.

"Gomez just turned the corner," Bishop said.

Hawke took a deep breath and continued stroking the pin tumblers with the rake pick. The keyway was sticky, probably as a result of dirt coming off from repeated insertions of the house key.

"At the door, good buddy," Bishop's voice came again in Hawke's ears a few minutes later. "He's taking out his keys."

Hawke forced himself to concentrate on the job. Several minutes passed, and then he heard the grinding sound of the elevator car descending to the lobby to pick up a passenger.

He knew that Gomez had just punched the elevator's down button. That gave two to five minutes more slack time, max.

Hawke soon heard the elevator motor hum again as the car began to ascend. Moments later he felt the final tumblers in the keyway line up, and with a twist of the tension wrench he rotated the cylinder plug to snap the bolt.

Twisting the doorknob, Hawke went inside the apartment and shut and locked the door behind him just as the sliding door of the elevator car retracted at the other end of the hallway.

It would be okay now, Hawke knew as he quickly took stock of the layout of the place. It was a three-room apartment, with the living room off to one side and the kitchen directly in front of him. The location of the kitchen wall phone was a key element in their plan.

Reaching beneath his sweatshirt, Hawke slid the silenced Beretta 93-R 9 mm machine pistol from the pit rig sprayed with Teflon lubricant for quick draws. He flipped off the safety. A hollowpoint was already nestled in the chamber.

A few pulse beats later Gomez turned the key in the first of the door's three snap locks.

Two more clicks, and the door began to open.

Crouching around the corner of the living room doorway, Hawke didn't see Gomez carry in a big brown grocery bag and drop it on the kitchen table. But he heard the phone ring a moment later.

Behind the wheel of the car parked on the street, Bishop held the cellular phone against the side of his face and heard the line pick up on the second ring.

"Yeah?" Gomez asked.

"Don't turn around," Hawke said, suddenly behind the smuggler. "Just hand me the phone. Slowly."

"What the hell—"

Gomez shut right up as he felt the cold steel of the silenced 93-R against the base of his spine and froze. Before he could even think of using the Smith and Wesson holstered under his brown bomber jacket, Hawke had him up against the wall.

"Two rings. I'll buzz you in," he said into the handset he'd taken from Gomez's limp fingers.

"Don't waste me, man," Gomez pleaded. "I got bucks. I can beat whatever Terra Nova paid you."

Frisking the dealer and assuring himself that he carried no other weapons besides the Smith & Wesson, Hawke used a plastic flex tie to bind his hands behind his back. Gomez was facedown on the kitchen linoleum when Bishop came in the door.

"He thinks Terra Nova sent us to whack him," Hawke said to Bishop.

"Where did he get that idea?" Bishop asked, squatting down beside the restrained dealer.

"Good question," Hawke returned. "How come you think Terra Nova sent us, Gomez?"

"Hey, I ain't dumb, man," answered the dealer, squirming on the linoleum. "Terra Nova put a contract out on me. And you ain't no cops. I can tell."

"You know, you are one very shrewd individual, Gomez," Bishop said without smiling. "But you're wrong about us coming to ice you. In fact, we want you alive and well."

"You telling me you're Feds?" Gomez asked in bewilderment.

"I'm telling you," Hawke said as he popped the tab off a can of beer taken from Gomez's grocery bag, "that we want you to play ball just like you told the Feds you would." He swallowed some suds and tossed a cold can to Bishop. "Because if you don't, my friend, we'll cut you loose and feed you to the great white shark.''

"What shark?" Gomez asked. "What the hell you talking about, man?"

They told him about Slater.

6

Slater bellied up to the Avis rental desk at La Guardia Airport, cutting in front of a businessman type in shirtsleeves who glared at him but knew better than to say anything to the big, tough-looking man.

He paid cash for a midsize Chrysler, barely flashing ID to the pretty brunette behind the desk and making sure the security cameras caught as little of his profile as possible.

He tooled the rental into the parking lot of a nearby motor inn and booked himself a room with a view...a view of the parking lot.

Sitting on the edge of the bed, he peeled the shrink-wrapping off the cap of a pint bottle of Jack Daniel's he'd picked up at the airport duty free and took a long slug of the Kentucky sour mash.

He slipped the half-full pint into his jacket pocket and put in another scrambled phone call to Guadalajara and ordered a clean piece, preferably a Steyr SSG-PIV sniper rifle, a silencer, preferably a Steyr accessory piece machined to fit its thread pattern, a sturdy carrying case for same and a box of hollowpoints.

In only a couple of hours, Slater found the large plastic shopping bag in the trunk of his rental car containing his order, including the Starlite scope he'd also put in for. Yes indeed, Terra Nova ran a tight ship—Slater had to hand it to him. The man seemed to have gofers hiding behind every bush.

SOON IT WAS starting to get dark. There was no moon, and even if there had been, the smog blowing across the river from Manhattan would probably have hidden it from view.

Slater chinked the grime-filmed blinds and scoped out the lot. It was standard issue, with its share of dense black spots between the halogens, pools of nothingness through which a shavetail fresh out of CIA fieldcraft 101 would have no trouble disappearing.

Just then Slater heard the rolling thunder overhead, which meant that one of the big 747s was coming in for a landing. He checked the watch at his wrist. He'd been timing the jets and could now estimate the rate of incoming planes at about one jetliner every three to four minutes.

Slater put on the soft felt hat with the droopy brim and the black cable-knit sweater he'd bought at the airport along with the alcohol. He left the motel through a fire door that gave access to the parking lot, paused to make sure he wasn't being watched, then walked casually to a car that wasn't his own but happened to be parked at one of the blind spots between the cones of light.

As the next jet thundered overhead, Slater dropped into the shadows and crouch-walked across a small weed-choked median strip until he was back on the airport outskirts again.

From there he made his way to the main terminal area and caught an express bus into Manhattan. He got off the bus at the Port Authority and rode the A-train into Brooklyn, switching to an uptown BMT train and then another until he was sure he wasn't being shadowed.

Slater disembarked at Grand Central Station and, using a special nontraceable access code, placed a call from a pay phone tucked away at the very end of the terminal's lower promenade.

In seconds he was on the blower to Mason Hawke. South of the border, down Mexico way, in Terra Nova's home turf, there was no secure method of holding such a conversation, but in New York it was another matter.

"We found the goods," Hawke said to Slater. He had the team's cellular phone unit pressed against his ear. Bishop and Hawke had Gomez on ice at a safe house across the Hudson in New Jersey.

"How does it go down?" Slater asked, keeping an eye on the subway commuters who trooped past him.

Hawke explained to Slater how they had set it up. Slater cradled the receiver, bought an apple turnover and walked away from the doughnut shop munching the pastry. He went into a nearby bookstore and browsed around the shelves, checking for surveillance.

After more countersurveillance moves he worked his way back to the motor inn by the reverse of the methods he'd used to leave it and retrieved the lethal hardware he'd stashed in his room.

GOMEZ WAS SITTING in the darkened South Bronx apartment watching Arsenio Hall on late-night TV. Slater crouched on the tar-papered rooftop of the tenement building across a narrow alleyway, two stories above the man who had been marked for death by Terra Nova.

Squinting through the Rank Pullin night scope mounted atop the Steyr SSG-PIV sniper rifle, Slater homed in on Gomez's chest. He knew that a lightweight vest of spun Kevlar fiber was worn underneath the dealer's clothes.

He also knew the body armor would stop the 7.62 x 51 mm slug fired by the Steyr but hoped that the bullet wouldn't break any ribs in the process. If he placed the shot right it wouldn't, and it didn't fit in with his plans to send Gomez to a hospital emergency room.

Slater squeezed off the round, compensating for the deflection of the bullet by windage and its passage through a glass windowpane. A pulse beat later a bright shower of red spurted from Gomez's chest as his body jerked violently and he toppled sideways onto the floor.

Slater dropped the rifle to the rooftop, climbed over the clay-tiled parapet and hustled down the fire escape. He hit the street and walked quickly to the rental car parked around the corner.

He was many blocks from the strike scene in seconds. By then heads were already popping out of open windows and residents were pointing in every direction. Gunshots were not unusual in this section of the South Bronx, but it still caused a stir when the shooting started.

Moments later a city ambulance came racing up to the apartment house. The two-man emergency service team pushed through the crowd that had gathered out front, hurried up the stairs and brought Gomez down on a stretcher. They shoved the bleeding man into the ambulance and sped away, sirens wailing.

"How'd I do?" Gomez asked inside the lurching vehicle.

"Not too good," replied Hawke, who was dressed in a paramedic uniform. He pulled away the bag of realistic red dye taped to Gomez's chest, which Slater's well-aimed round had burst apart, producing a lifelike shower of blood. "You're on your way out. In fact, you're gonna die before we reach the hospital."

THE FUNERAL SERVICE for Rudy Gomez was held the following day. Slater attended and, while nobody had told him, he knew that Terra Nova's eyes and ears were also watching and listening, checking out the proceedings for validity.

Slater caught a flight back to Guadalajara that same day. He'd had a one-minute phone conversation with Terra Nova at La Guardia airport to let him know the deed was done. The druglord took it in stride, but Slater knew the man was relieved. Deal Slater was to claim his reward for *una muerte de prueba* executed to perfection.

7

A predatory smile crossed Francisco Terra Nova's face. His hooded eyes couldn't conceal the cold, dangerous light that occasionally shot from their depths.

He held the gold spoon to his left nostril and inhaled some white cocaine powder. The spectacle below him was enthralling. Today's performance in the bullring would go down in the history of the sport, he sensed.

El Tiburon was the greatest matador since the immortal Manolito. He performed with masterful skill, egging the bull on, flirting with death as though it were a beautiful woman. Making love to it, in fact, making love to it and inviting its approach. El Tiburon was indeed a rare human being.

Now, with the lances of the *banderilleros* jostling in its back, the bull came on for his final charge before El Tiburon delivered the coup de grace.

Disdainfully—almost as though there were not several tons of mean, blood-crazed bull charging him—El Tiburon pivoted and faced the crowd, dropping the bright red cape in open defiance of the hate-crazed bull and letting it dangle maddeningly in his fist. At this point every spectator in the packed arena including Terra Nova went wild with applause.

Suddenly the bull was almost upon the matador. El Tiburon turned quickly and raised the gleaming sword high over his head. Sidestepping the bull, he thrust the long, keenly honed weapon into the thick muscle that bulged behind the bull's head.

The sword of the matador penetrated to the hilt. The bull stopped in midcharge. Its black eyes rolled up in its head, and its legs turned to rubber beneath the immense bulk of its tottering black body. The great animal collapsed at the bullfighter's feet, crashing to the dusty floor of the arena.

Hushed until now, the crowd erupted into a chorus of cheers and applause. Hundreds of flowers tossed from the stands came spilling down at El Tiburon, who raised his arms high in triumph.

Deal Slater stood beside Terra Nova and watched the spectacle. He had never understood the unique fascination that the bullring held for the Spanish psyche. The Superbowl, that was more his speed. But hell, thought Slater, to each his own.

After the matador had taken his final bows and left the arena, Terra Nova turned to Slater, his face flushed, his eyes wild.

"He was sublime, no?"

"Yeah," Slater said. "He sure had the moves."

"Magnificent," the druglord added, behaving as though he hadn't even heard Slater, choosing to ignore the sarcasm of the uncouth American. "You, too, have performed magnificently in your own field. That *maricon* Gomez could have brought down everything I've worked hard to achieve. I owe you something, my friend."

"You hired me to do a job," Slater said, his eyes watching workmen drag the carcass of the bull from the field and hose down the blood-soaked sands of the arena. "You paid your bill. You don't owe me squat."

"Perhaps. Then again, perhaps not," Terra Nova returned. "However, I didn't call you here to waste your time. I have another proposition for you. It involves a position with my organization as chief of security."

Slater shrugged, but the gesture masked the elation he felt. He had hoped that Terra Nova would nibble at the bait, and now the man had just bitten down hard on the hook. All Slater would have to do next was carefully reel in the druglord as if he were a prize marlin.

"Yeah, I can see how you'd need that," answered Slater curtly. "From what I've seen of your organization, you got more holes than a burrito has beans.

Against small-time *pistolas,* you're okay. But if you got bigger plans, look out, partner.''

"Precisely my thinking, Mr. Slater," Terra Nova replied. "I do indeed have larger plans for my organization. Stay at the Octagon a few days. We will talk further. In the meantime, *mi casa es tu casa.*"

SLATER LAY BACK on the comfortable bed. Night had fallen and the Octagon was still.

The stillness was deceptive, however. Terra Nova had a state-of-the-art electronic security system, as well as squads of armed men working around the clock to protect him from surprise attack.

Although Slater was tired, his plans for the night didn't call for sleep. He had just succeeded in jumping from the fringes of Terra Nova's operation into the first circle of its inner ranks. It was a short hop, but, all things considered, a major success.

Terra Nova might be a lot of things but he definitely wasn't stupid. Slater knew that the man was testing him, watching him, measuring and weighing him. Behind the engaging smile gaped the jaws of a shark. Behind the suave manner lurked the angel of death. If he screwed up, he'd be piranha bait quicker than he could say his own name.

But the risks went with the territory, and as far as Slater was concerned, a shot at busting up the Mexican's operation and setting things up for a follow-up strike on Carne in Colombia was worth whatever risks it took.

Slater had committed to memory the placement of the low-light TV cameras that ringed the Octagon. The surveillance cameras covered the grounds, but the security network, like all security networks, was not by any means goofproof.

Sliding back the high glass door on a narrow track, Slater stepped out onto the veranda fronting his room. A hot, humid breeze blew in from the nearby hills, carrying a sweetish scent of lush blooming jacaranda flowers mixed with the bitter smells of decaying vegetation. A cigarette flared below, the glowing orange pinpoint revealing to him the position of one of the guards patrolling the compound.

Slater remained standing motionless on the veranda. When the guard had disappeared from view, he swung out and dropped the fifteen feet to the ground below.

Speed and timing were everything now. Slater didn't know how long he could afford to be missing but estimated he had a half hour, max. He sprinted past the nearest camera as it swiveled away from him on a 180-degree pan and climbed a tree with a branch that overhung the security wall surrounding the Octagon, bypassing the motion sensors spaced at intervals along the top of the wall.

Keeping his profile low, Slater crouch-walked into the scrub and cactus that surrounded the estate. A few minutes later he came to the Mayan ruins where the specialized gear was to have been stashed by Hawke and Bishop.

They had worked out the placement of the gear before Slater went back to Mexico, having used satellite surveillance photos to pinpoint the location of the drop site because any aircraft passing overhead would be checked out and traced by Terra Nova's men.

Slater found the drop site after another five minutes' worth of search time. The PRC 319 HF/VHF burst-transmitter lay protected in a waterproof, thermally insulated pouch hidden amid the shattered rubble of the ancient Mayan ruins.

Suddenly he froze, hearing rubble dislodged behind him rolling down an incline. Slater whipped the H&K .38 pistol he wore under his jacket from shoulder leather, pivoting toward the source of the sound.

The ancient eyes met his. Unblinking reptilian eyes.

The rock iguana must have easily been four feet long. Slater had forgotten that they inhabited these ruins as though they were the ghosts of the ancient Mayans who had erected the stone edifices thousands of years before.

Holstering his piece, Slater went back to retrieving the drop transmitter. The pouch flap opened with the rasp of Velcro fasteners separating, and Slater removed the compact unit from its foam cocoon. He flipped on the power button and moments later saw the Ready message on the transmitter's narrow light-emitting diode screen.

Slater typed out the message on the unit's keyboard and saved it to memory. He played it back to satisfy himself that it was accurate, then hit the confirm key, followed by the send key.

The Transmission Successful message on the unit's screen confirmed that the report to Hawke and Bishop detailing Slater's forthcoming actions had been compressed into a high-frequency radio signal of a few seconds' duration.

There was no way for the signal to be deciphered, much less intercepted. Electronic handshaking protocols assured Slater that the Intelsat to which it was beamed had picked up the transmission and was already relaying it to the other two members of the SLAM strike team.

IN A VAN many miles from the drop site in the Mayan ruins, Hawke reacted to a beep-tone shrilling from his commo unit. Bishop was catching some shuteye in his chair and jerked awake as the down-linked message came in.

The van's rack-mounted high-speed computers and their UNIX-based software instantly decompressed and decrypted the coded transmission, which would have otherwise been unbreakable without the right software key even after months of effort.

"The transmission looks good," Hawke said to Bishop as a printer began spitting out hard copy. "We don't seem to be missing a byte." Then they brewed some coffee and got ready to implement the next phase of Operation Southern Star as they studied the breaking intelligence.

SLATER REPLACED the expensive piece of electronics in its storage pouch and yanked a pull string that released a highly corrosive acid into the interior of the pouch. He dropped the smoking polymerized sheath into a crevice in the rocks and heard the muffled thud as it hit bottom moments later.

The big gray-skinned iguana hardly moved a muscle as Slater passed it on extraction from the drop site. It only watched him with ancient yellow eyes, as though it had seen such activities a thousand times before.

8

Slater climbed up the drainpipe that ran down the side of the building wall and was soon back on the veranda fronting his guest room. He silently slid open one of the glass panels and reentered the room.

Somebody was already waiting inside it, somebody holding a gun on him. It was a small gun, a black .25-caliber Colt, but it could put a big enough hole in Slater just the same.

As his eyes adjusted to the darkness, Slater recognized the intruder as Venice, Terra Nova's girlfriend. She was wearing a thin kimono of shiny blue silk that barely concealed her large pink breasts and did nothing but show off her long, lean model's legs.

"Don't tell me you were out for a midnight swim," she began, "because there's nothing but sand for miles in any direction." A smile crossed the blonde's full lips, but the .25 stayed unwaveringly pointed at Slater.

"The dry heat's good for my sinuses," Slater responded.

"You look pretty healthy to me," Venice returned.

"I could ask you what you're doing in my room," Slater told her. He wasn't in the mood to dance. If she wanted to, fine. He'd take it a little bit further, but he wasn't going to dance with her all night.

Venice lowered the small pistol and dropped it into the pocket of her silk kimono.

"I didn't know it was you," she said. "I thought you were in bed."

"You still didn't say what you were doing here," Slater pressed.

Venice answered that question by sliding off the kimono and standing with her breasts and loins bared to his view. She approached him with her blue eyes locked on his and slid her arms around his neck.

"I wanted to have you," she said, and began to kiss him.

Slater pushed her away.

"Your boyfriend might not like that idea," he told her.

Venice wasn't about to be put off. She slithered back and rubbed up against Slater, pressing her naked body against his.

"Francisco doesn't care who I make it with. He gets off on me being with other men. But don't worry, I already asked him if I could have you."

"Maybe I better check it out with him myself," Slater insisted.

"Maybe I should tell Francisco I saw you climbing into your own window in the middle of the night."

This time Slater didn't push her away. Soon, with a triumphant laugh, she lay down on the bed and watched him with wide, hungry eyes.

"Take off your clothes," she whispered. "That's better," she continued a few minutes later as she ogled him coming toward her. "Now I'll call the shots."

Slater saw a calculating look in her eyes for a moment, along with the sultry come-hither look, as he knelt and began doing what Venice wanted of him while she moaned and thrashed her head from side to side.

"Yes!" she moaned soon. "Yes, that's the way!" Slater knew what was expected of him next and he was ready to give it to the blonde for as long as she wanted it.

He was locked together with her moments later, beginning the rhythmic thrust and counterthrust that built in speed and intensity until she sank her fingernails into his shoulders deep enough to draw blood and arched her body tautly beneath his.

Much later she shrugged her blue silk kimono back on and left the room. She didn't even give Slater a backward glance.

LATE THE FOLLOWING morning, Slater climbed into the Toyota four-by-four beside the taciturn Montana. They set off to take care of some important business for Terra Nova.

The druglord was doing a coke deal on his own hook, without the involvement of Carne, his usual Colombian supplier. Slater's destination was a small private airfield nearby, where a Lockheed Lodestar 18 twin-engine plane was standing by to shuttle them toward a drop zone where the dope would be transshipped.

The coke run, set up on the other end by Ñandú, a long-time and trusted connection, was coming to Terra Nova by way of a fast boat from the port of Champerico, a dot on the Guatemala side of the Mexican border.

The coke run would proceed up the Pacific along the Mexican coast, and the drop would go down on one of the remote beaches of Manzanillo, less than a hundred miles from Terra Nova's home base at Guadalajara.

Slater had plans of his own regarding the drop, plans that he'd already transmitted via burst commo equipment to his two SLAM teammates. He was sure that Hawke and Bishop were already taking care of business on their own end.

How his two teammates handled the challenge was important to the success or failure of the mission. Of the Mutt-and-Jeff act that made up Terra Nova's two most trusted bodyguards, the one called Montana was the only one with any brains. Delgado was just a throwaway. Therefore Montana was the only player who could spell trouble for the operation.

What this added up to was that Montana had to take a fall. The best way Slater could figure to achieve such an objective would be to have him taken down in the upcoming coke drop.

This played right into the event stream of the unfolding operation. Montana's sudden demise would be the perfect way to inject the critical spear point that would open up Terra Nova's organization to deeper penetration.

The only wild card now was Venice. Slater realized that the lady could be potentially dangerous to the successful outcome of the strike against Terra Nova. A borderline case though she might be, she'd seen him doing something he'd had no business doing. Now she knew too much for her own good.

Slater would just have to wait and see what he'd do about Venice.

9

The EC-3A airborne warning and control system—AWACS—plane cruised at a flight ceiling of eleven thousand feet over the placid waters of the southwestern Pacific.

The AWACS plane was normally assigned to the Southern Command of U.S. counternarcotics activities, scouring the air and sea lanes lying between Caribbean island republics and the United States for drugrunners in fast boats and light aircraft.

Now the electronic surveillance platform had been hastily pulled from its regular patrol zone to engage in a priority-coded mission.

Inside the equipment-crammed interior of the aircraft, U.S. Customs signals Intelligence officers were bathed in the soft red light of multiple data screen arrays.

The screens were linked to radar aerials housed in the saucer-shaped rotodome fixed atop the fuselage just aft of the aircraft's wings. The equipment was capable of tracking hundreds of bogies simultaneously.

Data from the airborne tracking station was normally channeled to U.S. Customs and Coast Guard interception units participating in the multinational and interagency communications and Intelligence program.

But tonight's mission was unique in that the EC-3A platform was acting as flying lookout for a single, specialized target. This was a cabin cruiser expected to be encountered on the Champerico-to-Manzanillo drug-running corridor.

When was not known, nor was where. The single clear factor was that it would be mobile tonight within a thousand-square-mile stretch of open ocean.

The electronic eye in the sky constantly scanned the sea lanes of the Pacific below, alert for the fast-moving needle in the haystack.

The human operators who scanned the observation aircraft's instrumentation banks were assisted by high-speed computers that filtered raw data fed into them by the EC-3A's radar, matching known parameters against the observed maritime traffic. If anyone was capable of picking up the smuggler's boat, the crew of the EC-3A could.

At 0045 a three-note alarm at one of the scanning consoles signaled the attending officer that the computers had spotted a likely contender. High-speed electronic interrogation revealed that the fast, sleek craft was traveling at thirty-five knots. Its projected destination was the coast of southwestern Mexico.

"Sir, I've got a possible," the officer relayed to the EC-3A's mission commander.

"Be right there," the mission commander replied via internal commo from his station up front.

Minutes later both men were monitoring the glowing red icon on the radar scope, which had appeared on the VDT's northeast sector.

"Looks like she's really traveling," the crew chief told the technician. "Good going. Log the sighting per your instructions."

The officer inputted a command sequence that transmitted the coordinates of the oceangoing craft to the radio officer.

At the nose of the aircraft, the radio officer received the data and activated the secure communications link to the *Blue Ridge*, a U.S. Navy frigate anchored off the shore of Mexico's Isla de Revillagigedo.

Minutes after reception of the secure coded telemetry, Mason Hawke and Eddie Bishop were summoned from their bunks aboard the frigate and informed that the target vessel had been sighted and was currently being tracked on its course by the EC-3A plane.

THE TIME WAS now 0134 hours.

Hawke and Bishop were already suited up and ready

to go. Their black nylon action togs were rigged out with mil spec load-bearing suspenders on which were festooned an array of weapons, commo gear and survival equipment.

Up on the helipad located on the aft deck of the *Blue Ridge,* a Blackhawk helicopter was warming up prior to takeoff, its rotors spinning slowly.

Hawke and Bishop climbed aboard the coptor's port and starboard hatchways. They signaled to the pilot that they were ready for immediate takeoff.

The Hawk pilot flashed the two men the thumbs-up. Hydraulic pressure had climbed and stabilized, and the "chiclets" on his instrumentation panel were going green. Engine one, then two, roared to life.

Pulling pitch, the pilot made the Hawk spread its wings and take to the black sky on its night hunt. The Blackhawk's four rotors pulled the heavy aircraft to an altitude of five feet off the flight deck of the frigate.

At that point the Hawk achieved transitional lift and rose straight up to thirty feet with the speed of an express elevator.

The pilot logged course coordinates into the Blackhawk's navigational system. AN/PVS-7A night-observation equipment gave him the ability to fly the chopper without lights in a wide range of weather conditions.

Aft of the main pilot's area at the nose of the aircraft, Hawke and Bishop were also donning night-vision gear.

The goggles strapped to their heads utilized third-generation light-amplification technology. Built-in antibloom safeguards ensured that their night vision would remain intact even in the midst of an all-out firefight.

Deployed at the starboard hatch of the Blackhawk a GE Minigun was mounted. The Minigun was capable of firing six thousand 7.62 mm rounds per minute and had proven itself time and time again in Nam and in every major confrontation since.

Bishop checked the 30-round clip of the Colt Commando SMG he ported. Its compact dimensions, combined with the firepower of a true autorifle, made the short-barreled 5.56 mm assault weapon the natural choice for use in the cramped surroundings of a helicopter.

The two SLAM bangers were ready to take down the boat.

THE CREW OF THE fast vessel, a Chris Craft cabin cruiser, had passed the midway point on their smuggler's run. They could now clearly discern the lights of Acapulco shimmering off to port.

So far so good, thought the skipper. He was *un apuntido,* one of the "enlisted ones" who made their living on the periphery of the drug trade. He was a veteran smuggler, and the run from Champerico to Manzanillo wasn't new to him. He had made the same run dozens of times before.

The two *Indios* at the stern were another matter. They were Ñandú's *pistolas*. Cutthroats and scum recruited from the boondocks.

They thought the M-16s they carried made up for the fact that they were stupid. They thought that thirty bullets in the clip made up for no brains in the head. They were dumb *cholos,* thought the skipper.

On top of being stupid, Ñandú's two *pistolas* were drunk, too. They had been guzzling cheap rum since practically the first moment they had come aboard the skipper's boat. They stank of the rotgut.

The skipper had kept to himself in the wheelhouse and had made certain that the 9 mm Browning at his hip was cleaned, oiled and ready to use against those two stinking *Indios* at the back of the boat.

Ñandú had told the skipper that his two buttonmen were coming along to protect him. The skipper had wondered aloud who would protect him from *them.* He argued against having them on board, but Ñandú had insisted. In the end there was no choice but to agree.

Suddenly a shout came from the rear of the boat. One of Ñandú's men was screaming and pointing frantically toward the sky. The skipper poked his head through the open window of the wheelhouse, but everything appeared normal.

He shouted out toward the stern, asking what all the commotion was about. He could see nothing, hear nothing, except for the roar of his boat's engines and the steady slap of the prow knifing through the choppy sea.

The two *Indios* aft weren't paying the skipper any attention, though. They were raising their autorifles and pointing them up at the blackness of the sky.

The skipper believed they had gone loco, but then he heard the telltale chugging of helicopter rotor blades overhead. Squinting skyward, the skipper could now finally discern the outline of the chopper against the clouds.

The skipper unleathered his 9 mm pistol, crossed himself and uttered an oath. Ñandú had screwed him proper this time.

10

Image-intensification technology disclosed the presence of the fast smuggler's boat despite the less than optimum viewing conditions prevailing in the pitch darkness of the predawn hours.

"Cut your engines, stand to and prepare for immediate boarding," the Hawk pilot's amplified voice boomed down from the black night sky.

Instead of heeding the command, the skipper of the smuggler vessel pulled out the throttle and tried to hightail it out of the area. The boat's turbocharged, after-cooled two-stroke diesel engines were fast but not nearly fast enough to outrun the Blackhawk.

"This is your final warning," the pilot repeated, night-vision technology giving him a precise visual fix on the position of the craft. "Cut your engines and stand to. Failure to obey this order will result in immediate action."

The sudden blue muzzle-flashes of small-arms automatic fire originating from the aft deck of the cabin cruiser was the pilot's final answer.

Such a response had been expected, but conventions of maritime law required the issuance of a warning. That warning having been duly given, it was now time for SLAM to kick some ass.

Hawke was already strapped in behind the Minigun, the elastic webbing giving him flexibility of movement that allowed him to efficiently sight and target the motorized 7.62 mm machine gun.

Bishop was rough-spotting the Commando 5.56 mm subgun through the weapon's open sights as the Blackhawk banked and swung in on a steeply angled intercept vector.

Thanks to the capabilities of the night-vision goggles they wore, both SLAM personnel had no difficulty whatever in viewing the escaping craft despite the complete absence of mission lights and the ambient darkness of the night. They enjoyed complete tactical superiority and would exploit this edge to the maximum.

While the automatic-weapons fire that lashed up at them from the speeding vessel was inaccurate, SLAM's answering steel would be right on target. If the two shooters on the boat thought they were involved in a pissing contest, they were dead wrong.

The pilot swung the chopper in on a low-angle trajectory that brought Hawke broadside of the two gunmen on the cruiser's aft deck. The Minigun wailed and bucked as its motor-driven multiple barrels revolved at a high-speed blur.

The human target below was struck repeatedly with heavy-caliber 7.62 mm slugs across the upper chest region, inflicting massive physical trauma.

Flinging out his arms and dropping his weapon, the man went down, tried to crawl, then collapsed into a helpless jumble of flailing arms and scissoring legs.

As the Blackhawk veered overhead, Bishop cut loose with a 5.56 mm autoburst from the Commando, raking the deck with fifty rounds of full-metal-jacketed tumblers and terminating the second gunman with the speed of a fly caught in the flame of a blowtorch.

One pass was all it took to make short work of Ñandú's two triggermen. As for the boat's skipper, he was a man who knew when the game was zero-sum. As soon as he saw that Ñandú's two torpedoes were out of commission, he throttled down and cut his engines.

Now the pilot switched on the Blackhawk's powerful searchlight beacon. In the intense white glare of the copter's beam the spread-eagled corpses of the gunmen at the stern were revealed amid splatters of spilled blood and the pockmarks from hundreds of bullets. Up toward the prow in the wheelhouse, the frightened skipper could be seen with his hands up in the air, blinking furiously as he faced into the light.

"Do not move," the pilot commanded the skipper via loud-hailer. "Do not use the radio. Remain standing where you are until you are told to do otherwise."

The pilot manipulated collective and cyclic pitch controls, and the chopper dropped like a stone until it was hovering only a few feet from the deck, stabilized by its tail rotor.

Hawke and Bishop jumped down from the port and starboard personnel hatchways and raced quickly toward the wheelhouse while the Blackhawk gained altitude, banked sharply and sped without lights back to the *Blue Ridge,* its role in the night mission completed.

While Bishop dumped the two corpses overboard into the briny deep, Hawke faced the terror-stricken skipper.

"Please, no!" he pleaded. "I am no *pistola.* I skipper a boat. Nothing more."

"You play ball with us, *compadre,"* Hawke told him, "and we treat you right, okay?"

"Si, si!" he shouted. "Whatever you want, whatever you say."

Hawke wondered if the frightened smuggler would really play ball or if he would balk when he realized that his dues would entail giving up Ñandú's stash.

"First the dope stash," Hawke said. "Where is it?"

The skipper directed him to a locker with markings indicating it contained life jackets and preservers. He said the dope was stashed in a false bottom.

Hawke made him open it himself. It wasn't that hard to booby-trap a stash, he knew.

Inside the secret compartment, sealed in seventy-five two-kilo oblong bags, SLAM found the real McCoy. Coke, uncut and pure as the driven snow, with a wholesale value of two million dollars on the street.

"Hey, you know what, amigo?" Bishop told the sweating skipper. "You look like a guy we can do a deal with."

SLATER SAT on the windswept heights above the gray sands of Manzanillo Beach, scanning the black ocean through the glowing green field of night-observation binoculars. Beside him was a luggage case full of neatly banded and stacked bills in large denominations amounting to five hundred grand. Arrayed on either side of him were a dozen of Terra Nova's *pistolas,* who had accompanied himself and Montana to the drop site.

By now Slater figured that the SLAM strike team had located and boarded the boat sent by the Guatemalan. According to plan, Hawke and Bishop would follow through with the dope drop, which would proceed as planned, except for the fact that the two SLAM personnel would be on board the cruiser.

Slater would have to be ready for their arrival. The dope drop was scheduled to come off precisely at 0500 hours, and this fateful moment was only minutes away.

Right on schedule, lights came on and off in the off-shore darkness. This was the signal that Ñandú's boatload of coke was approaching the beach. One long, one short, one long, the flashes came.

The *pistolas* on the sandy heights with Slater were excited at the approach of the boat, in much the same way dogs get excited by the promise of meat. They were up and running toward the shore, waving their rifles to attract the attention of those on board the incoming craft. More sober than the rest, Montana hefted his massive frame up from the sands and produced a flashlight from the pocket of his jacket.

Aiming the torch at the source of the offshore signal, he flashed the recognition code that they'd just received from the boat in reverse sequence. One short, one long, one short.

Minutes later the silhouette of the cruiser was visible as it slid through the black waters of the Pacific toward the rocky shore. The boat came right up to the beach. Against the starlit horizon the outlines of men were visible on board.

Men with guns.

Hawke and Bishop positioned themselves to port and starboard aft of the wheelhouse and opened fire on the reception committee gathered on the beach. The plan was to make it look like a double cross by Ñandú while at the same time taking down Montana and removing Terra Nova's right-hand man from the overall picture.

As expected, Terra Nova's *pistolas* were caught napping. They dropped left and right under the fusillade of buzz-sawing lead.

Because Montana stood at the shoreline, he was right in the line of fire and was among the first to be hit. The mammoth gunman went down in a lurching, blood-spraying heap while his men scattered in all directions.

Slater ducked down behind the cover of a stone outcrop and pulled a Mini-Uzi SMG from a quick-action Velcro shoulder rig worn under his windbreaker. He launched a volley of automatic fire at the boat, angling the burst in close enough to force Hawke and Bishop to duck for cover.

They in turn countered with bursts of 5.56 mm suppressing fire from Bishop's Colt Commando and the Ultimax machine gun now ported by Hawke. Both Slater and the two SLAM agents on board had to make the performance look real for the benefit of Terra Nova's torpedoes.

Grabbing the luggage case full of buy money after launching another burst from the Uzi, Slater shouted at the surviving *pistolas* to beat a path for the two four-by-fours that had brought them to the drop site.

They didn't need much prompting to pile into the trucks and take off, or to leave the fallen Montana behind on the blood-soaked sands of Manzanillo Beach.

11

"Ñandú is a dead man!" roared Terra Nova. Slater had never seen the man worked up like this before.

An insane fury gripped him. His entire body shook. His eyes rolled in his head like painted steel balls as he pounded his fists down on his desk. "He wants war! All right! I'll give him war!"

Terra Nova wanted Slater to immediately organize and execute a devastating strike on Ñandú.

It would be worth fifty grand up front and another fifty as a completion bonus to Slater if he wiped out Ñandú's narcotics-processing operation on the Guatemala border.

Terra Nova told Slater to immediately put together a unit assembled from his army of torpedoes and lead them south on a search-and-destroy mission.

"None of your men," Slater countered right away, shaking his head. "Myself and two others. That's all I'll need."

"What?" Terra Nova returned in shock and disbelief. "Three men against Ñandú's private militia? Assaulting an armed encampment? Are you crazy, gringo?''

"Not crazy," Slater shot back. "But not stupid enough to risk my neck with the likes of your piss-ant soldiers, either. The two men I have in mind are the best that money can buy. Like myself, they're former Delta. On the best day of their lives your men aren't even fit to wipe their asses."

The drug honcho considered Slater's proposition for a minute. His hands flexed and unflexed on his desk. His nostrils flared and a muscle on his throat twitched repeatedly. Terra Nova was one very wrapped-tight man, Slater realized. A man on the verge of explosion.

"Okay," he told Slater after a while, now unwinding and flashing his security chief a broad grin. "You handle it your way. Just remember one thing. You blow this payback, you make me look like a piece of shit. People I deal with get the idea I'm weak, I get ripped off again. Do you understand what I am telling you, amigo?"

Slater nodded.

"Ñandú is going to pay," he solemnly said to Terra Nova. "You have my word on it. He is going to pay some heavy coin for fucking you over."

THE NIGHT WAS MOONLESS. The waters off the Pacific coast were a calm, seamless black. Cruising low above the placid ocean with the three strikers on board, the prop aircraft skimmed the surface of the sea, flying "under the curtain" on a radar-evading flight path.

Slater had chartered the Dehavilland amphibious plane in Texas. The plane had a cruising range of over eleven hundred miles and a reserve fuel load that could almost double that figure. It was capable of setting down either on water or on land, its underwing-mounted pontoons giving it the capability to remain afloat even in rough seas.

In the darkened cockpit lit only by the soft green glow of instrumentation terminals, Slater checked the Dehavilland's navigational controls.

Linked to a Navstar satellite in low orbit and using a GPS, or global positioning system, the on-board computer followed the radio beacon to the coordinates programmed into its silicon brain. Estimated remaining flight time was one hour and fifteen minutes.

While Slater piloted the Dehavilland, Hawke and Bishop were stationed in the cabin aft of the cockpit, putting the gear they had brought along through a final mud check, cleaning every surface, loading every mag, counting every round.

The three "mercs" in Terra Nova's employ had no trouble requisitioning the weapons, ordnance and supplies they had requested for deployment on the payback raid. The druglord's millions of illicit narcodollars could buy anything available on the arms market.

The strike team was outfitted with sound-suppressed Heckler & Koch MP-5 submachine guns for Hawke and Bishop. Slater, too, would carry an H&K equipped with a silencer but with the addition of an Oldelft night scope.

Packs of demolition ordnance included blocks of C-4 plastic explosive, detonators and grenades. German-made Panzerfaust Pzf-3 antiarmor rockets were also available, improved and modernized versions of the Nazi army's World War II tank busters standardly equipped with 110 mm HEAT warheads and shoulder-fire capable.

Outfitted with state-of-the-art combat gear, the three-man infiltration and destruction crew was more than equal to anything that Ñandú's drug money could buy.

Hawke went forward and slid into the copilot's seat beside Slater. The SLAM honcho was keeping an eye on the glowing instrumentation panel in front of him while continuously checking out the water below, the sky above and the horizon up ahead.

Hawke handed Slater a steaming cup of coffee from the thermos they had brought on board at the airfield outside of Brownsville, Texas, where they'd taken off. Slater drank his java black, no sugar, using one hand.

He didn't speak with Hawke. His mind had drifted back to other night missions that had taken place during the Hundred Hour War in Iraq.

Mixed Delta and SAS units were tasked with the job of infiltrating into Iraq and taking out mobile and fixed Scud launchers, which were posing threats to coalition member countries.

Hercules aircraft flown by the U.S. First Special Operations Wing and carrying U.S.-British teams kept in constant readiness to drop SOF elements into the strike zones as soon as reconnaissance aircraft, spy satellites or signals intelligence had located the installations. Extraction was accomplished by PAVE LOW III choppers.

As the desert war hotted up, Slater's Scud-hunter teams were also tasked with rescue and recovery of downed pilots, illuminating targets for laser-guided bombs and busting up triple-A installations too hard to be taken down by any other means except by forces deployed on the ground.

In all these operations, two men had distinguished themselves by their resourcefulness, courage and smarts. When the conflict was settled and the orders from the White House establishing the elite and ultrasecret three-man SLAM strike force were handed down—a force based on a similar tactical formation first deployed by MACV/SOG in Vietnam—Slater knew that the two men he would select for further training would be Hawke and Bishop.

Slater had chosen Hawke and Bishop because they were the best of the best. In a special off-limits area of Delta's Stockade at Bragg and at selected sites around the world duplicating terrain and environmental features of projected action zones, he had trained them personally for the unique shock-warfare operational scenarios they would be likely to face.

Search, Locate and Annihilate Missions would be mounted to destroy the threat posed by multinational, multitiered drug conspiracies with SLAM as a razor-edged spear point striking at the heart of the narco-barons' most vulnerable assets.

Dictators like Saddam Hussein were in some ways less dangerous than the hidden manipulators who trafficked in drugs to amass immense fortunes but whose ultimate aims were power for its own sake.

The breakup of the former East Bloc satellites had deepened the pool of high-quality pawns, knights and bishops available to the world's clandestine chess masters on the free-lance operative market.

The players were everywhere. Subwarfare—intense, violent and unseen in the shadow world of covert operations—was the shape of things to come.

Tonight's hit on Ñandú's warehouse on the Mexico-Guatemala border was small change compared to the task of shutting down gigantic narcoconspiracies, the reason why SLAM had been activated in the first place.

It was true that hundreds of millions of dollars in street value worth of coke would be destroyed in the raid. But Slater had no illusions about the strike's ultimate effects on drug trafficking in general. The absence of hundreds of kilos of pure snow wouldn't even put a small dent in the quantity of drugs available on the street.

For SLAM the raid was only a sideshow. No more, no less. The main events—drug traffickers like Terra Nova and his Colombian partner, Rogelio la Carne— were the actual targets of the operation. Blowing the Guatemalan coke laboratory to hell and gone would merely be SLAM's way of getting out of the peanut gallery and into the main arena.

Soon the Dehavilland's navigational system beeped.

SLAM was approaching the strike zone.

Slater switched off the automatic-pilot feature and got behind the plane's controls. It was time to bring the Dehavilland in for a landing. He nosed the amphibious aircraft down toward the glassy surface of the black-green sea.

12

Compressed air from high-pressure cylinders inflated the large rubber raft in a matter of minutes. Fully inflated, the Zodiac was easily large enough to accommodate the three-man strike team, as well as a full mission load of precision combat gear.

Hawke fitted the specially silenced outboard engine onto the rubber raft and punched the start button. Slater and Bishop were already on board.

The action togs that the three strikers wore were woven of nonreflective black nylon fabric. The lethal tools of their trade hung from webbing. Their faces were cammied with nonreflective paint, and black watch caps covered their heads.

With Hawke acting as helmsman, the craft plowed silently and speedily through the calm sea toward the shore of Tapachula, a beachhead situated a few miles from the port of Champerico, where the cruiser seajacked by SLAM had initially sailed from.

Slater and Bishop reconnoitered the sea and land that lay to the port bow of the strike team's inflatable target infiltration craft. Using GEN-III night-vision binoculars, they scanned the mission zone dead ahead for evidence of sentry activity.

A heavy night surf pounded the rocky shoreline, and the swaying of windblown beach grass provided the only manifestations of activity. They detected no sign of sentinels on the sands.

Now the beachhead loomed up ahead. It was a crescent-shaped area strewn with boulders, and it gave way to low rocky bluffs a few yards from the waterline. No craft of any kind was visible on the sea except for the dark bulking mass of the amphibious Dehavilland securely anchored far from shore.

Hawke expertly piloted the Zodiac toward a spot on the beach zone well screened from view of the land by trees growing amid a jumble of boulders. As they approached the LZ, the three SLAM strikers donned Anvis night-vision goggles and adjusted them for optimum brightness.

After beaching the black rubber dinghy in a site sheltered by rocks and vegetation, Slater, Hawke and Bishop crossed the strip of boulder-littered beach, alert for hidden mantraps and antipersonnel devices.

First Slater scaled the low rocky bluff above the beach, followed by the other two SLAM commandos. Visible no more than a few hundred yards ahead of them was Ñandú's coke-production facility. The main structure was a large, tin-roofed shed about thirty feet in length and ten feet across.

Stacked nearby were fifty-five-gallon steel drums containing the flammable ethyl ether used in the process by which raw coca was cooked down and ultimately converted to cocaine base.

Other tin-roofed structures—longhouses a third as large as the main facility, and a few smaller sheds—were the only other buildings located within the compound that was encircled by a crude barbed-wire perimeter fence.

An observation platform stood thirty feet above the south corner of the base, near which several four-by-fours were parked. The watchtower was crewed by two sentries armed with AK-47 automatic rifles.

Crouch-walking across the sandy ground, the three strikers approached the perimeter fence. Communicating silently by means of hand signals, Slater indicated that he would take out the sentries deployed in the crow's nest.

Hawke and Bishop would split up, deal with whatever base personnel they encountered and slot the C-4 demo charges, which would be timed to detonate simultaneously.

SLATER UNSHIPPED wire cutters and snipped through the strands of barbed wire that formed the coke installation's perimeter fence. Inside the fence he paused for a few seconds and scanned the compound's interior, alert for any sign that he had been spotted.

He listened to the chugging of a gas-powered electric generator, the barking of dogs and the tinny sounds of a radio playing marimba music from somewhere deeper inside the compound.

Considering it safe to proceed, Slater edged laterally toward the foot of the steel tower supporting the crow's nest. Long minutes of patient, slow movement passed before Slater reached the structure's base. Above him he could now hear the lookouts as they conversed in rapid Spanish.

The lookouts were not professionals. They were more of the standard-issue *pistolas* of the same type he'd encountered before, civilians playing soldier but far out of their depth.

Silhouetted against the night, they were presenting themselves as perfect targets for a sniper attack and they didn't even realize it. They were cheap talent, fated to have a short life span in the merc game.

Crouching, Slater unshipped the Heckler & Koch MP-5 SMG equipped with an Oldelft MS4GT IR scope. There was already a 9 mm hollownose chambered.

The stubby profile of the Hush Puppy silencer projecting from the muzzle of the weapon increased its barrel length by several inches. Inside the cylinder, concentric washers would bleed off the hot gases for controlled discharge of its ammo load.

Although the Hush Puppy would silence the report of discharging rounds and suppress muzzle-flash, it wouldn't degrade the accuracy of the weapon by a significant factor. Taking out both sentries with the weapon was doable, Slater decided.

Crouched in the darkness, Slater sighted the MP-5 on the first sentry centered in the night scope's white target reticle. He squeezed off a low-decibel parabellum round, and the sentry's head vanished in a smudge of crimson.

The other sentry froze in place as the first merc lurched backward, but Slater's second bullet caught him, too, as it noiselessly tore away most of his throat and lower jaw, spinning him around in a half turn to land dangling over the edge of the crow's nest.

Cradling the SMG, Slater crossed the compound at a flat-out run. The background chugging of the gas generator that supplied power to the facility had drowned out the sounds of the lookout takedowns and masked those of Slater's movements.

His primary target was the stacks of fifty-five-gallon ether drums. They were located in a big warehouse shed placed as far from the main refinery area as possible because of the high danger of explosion they presented.

Unshipping the blocks of plastic explosive compound, Slater planted the C-4 cubes in the sandy ground. Into each block of plastic explosive he inserted the stainless-steel cylinder of a chronoelectronic fuze.

He programmed the fuze by means of a thin-edged hand-held Bressel electronic programmer that displayed the detonation time on a backlit LCD strip. When he had wired all the charges, Slater moved silently toward the main processing shed.

He would have to proceed more carefully now. Crossing from the drum storage area to the refinery shed would involve negotiating the central portion of the camp.

Crouching to keep his profile low and confining himself to the dark areas between buildings, Slater began moving toward the shed. He had pushed the NVG tubes up over his face in order to use his normal vision. Because the NVGs were state-of-the-art, Slater experienced only a second or two of transition time before his vision adjusted.

Entering the large shed, he saw scattered solvent drums, processing vats and drying tables, as well as gunnysacks and bales of coca leaves piled almost to the roof of the shed.

The overpowering stench of the cocaine residue was heavy in the sluggish tropical air. Slater began moving heaps of coca-filled burlap sacks when he realized that there was a slumbering guard who had made his bed on one of them.

The guard awoke suddenly, his bloodshot eyes glazed with sleep and big with fear. He grabbed for the AK-47 rifle beside him but was unsure whether to fire the gun or to yell for help.

Slater acted quickly, not giving the guard a chance to pull his wits together. The silenced MP-5 at his hip coughed twice and blew the guard into the sack of coca in a bloodied heap.

Slater unshipped four more of the plastic charges. Working quickly, he slotted each of the blocks of C-4 at compass points across the length and width of the refinery and armed them as he had done with the previous cluster. Completing the task in just under three minutes, he slipped back into the concealment of the shadows surrounding the shed.

13

Mason Hawke heard the congested gurgle from the sentry's throat as air escaped from lungs rapidly filling with hot arterial blood. He allowed the limp body to slowly crumple to the sandy ground.

Hawke withdrew the bloodstained Ka-Bar commando knife from the throat of the terminated sentinel and dragged the corpse into the concealment of a jacaranda thicket, then stowed the dead merc's Valmet assault rifle alongside its former wielder.

Guided by night-vision goggles, Hawke dogtrotted toward his designated target, the facility's barracks longhouse. Pale light from naked bulbs spilled from windows and seeped from the crack beneath the nearest of the two doors at either end. Inside the dormitory Ñandú's *coqueros* were sweating out another hot, humid night in the jungle.

The structure was supported on beams, with a two-foot crawl space between the floor planking and the ground as protection against periodic flooding. Unfortunately for the *coqueros* within the bunkhouse, the arrangement would not do the same for high-explosive blast effect. Sliding under the dormitory, Hawke unshipped his time-fuzed charges from musette bags at his waist and slotted them under the building at intervals of five feet.

Completing the demo job, he slid out from under the barracks and crossed to the second of the crude structures situated a few feet away. This one was a smaller wooden building that functioned as the base mess and administrative quarters.

It was deserted now except for an old mongrel dog that wandered by, sniffed at Hawke's leg, then disappeared into the night, wagging its tail. Hawke jimmied the lock on the door and searched inside the darkened room beyond, noticing through his goggles a sign in Spanish, which read Cleanliness Is A Virtue. In a drawer of a steel desk he found low-level documents, mostly bills for goods and services provided to the base by local contractors. Hawke pocketed the papers before slotting more charges throughout the building.

As HAWKE WAS exfiltrating the structure on his way to SLAM's rally point, Bishop was nearing the installation's motor pool area.

A merc in camouflage fatigues was leaning against a pickup truck, an unlit cigarette slanted between his lips. The flaring of his match as he lit up the butt revealed strong Indian features and a scruffy beard.

Bishop shot him tap-tap style with the sound-suppressed MP-5 SMG studded on single-shot mode—two rounds right between the eyes as the SAS had taught Delta to do it. The terminated sentinel flopped backward across the hood of the truck, then slid down to his knees, his mouth open in the final surprise of death.

Bishop shoved the body underneath one of the four-by-fours parked in the lot. He slotted a magnetically attached charge beneath each of the trucks close to the fuel tank, set the digital timers and vanished back into the predawn shadows.

HAVING COMPLETED their individually assigned tasks, Slater, Hawke and Bishop extracted and linked up at their rendezvous point. They hustled from the base compound toward the edge of the low bluffs fronting the beach zone. There Slater unshipped a pair of compact night-vision binoculars and consulted his Tag-Huer, which confirmed that the charges were set to blow in minutes.

From a gear pouch Bishop took a compact 8 mm video camera equipped with a long-range telephoto lens and got it ready to shoot what would go down as soon as Slater triggered the charges.

In another place and time, Terra Nova might have demanded some ears or fingers or genitals as proof of what had taken place, but video technology had changed all that.

Terra Nova wanted something he could enjoy on his wide-screen TV with a snifter of brandy and a couple of lines of nose candy for company.

Bishop signaled that he was ready to roll them, and Slater watched the elapsed-time window on his chronometer, mentally counting down. Dozens of charges went ballistic all at once as the LCD readout flashed a solid row of zeros.

Bahhh-looom!

A split second after the bright detonation flash lit up the darkness, the blast's shock wave and broiling heat moved through the night.

Then came a wall of searing air displaced by the explosion as tongues of hot orange flame licked up at the swollen black underbelly of the cloud-filled sky from points all across the compound.

Those charges that Slater had slotted out by the fifty-five-gallon ether drums ignited the highly flammable fluid and sent it spraying skyward in enormous fiery geysers.

A blazing inferno straight out of hell quickly engulfed the entire coke-processing facility.

Soon the continual booming of the explosions and the express-train roar of the vortexing flames sucking gouts of air into their churning centers was mingled with the blood-chilling screams of Ñandú's men as they poured in a many-voiced frenzy from the burning barracks longhouses where they had been asleep only minutes before.

Masses of crackling, spluttering flames enveloped the doomed men. They dashed about frantically, human firebrands who hurled themselves to the ground in desperate attempts to quench the hellfire consuming their flesh and igniting the marrow in their bones.

But their violent flopping and thrashing brought no end to their suffering. Only death could grant relief, and soon dozens of burnt corpses littered the fire-scorched earth, smoking and charred, soft and pink on one side, crisp and black on the other.

Twenty minutes later the three-man strike unit had reboarded the Dehavilland. The amphibious aircraft's powerful fuel-injector engines propelled the pontoon plane forward, and it gained lift in seconds.

Slater banked the Dehavilland in a shallow arc above the surface of the wind-whipped sea and pointed her nose north, toward Mexico.

14

Francisco Terra Nova stared at the hundred-inch TV screen with hypnotic fascination. He had played back the video footage of the destruction of Ñandú's dope base dozens of times. He couldn't get enough of it.

Now he ran the tape one final time in the privacy of his stateroom. He found the sequence of pulsed explosions and their fiery aftermath riveting. It was almost better than watching an American porn flick.

When he'd had too much of his good thing, Terra Nova zapped off the video and exited the stateroom. Walking down the narrow companionway, he heard the muted sounds of American-style rock music and the occasional burst of near-hysterical, drug-fueled laughter coming from the party on the deck topside.

He would soon join the festivities himself. Indeed, he would have to put in an appearance, or those of his guests who were less inebriated might start asking where their host was hiding himself. For the present, though, Terra Nova looked forward to a special form of entertainment that was for his pleasure alone.

As he had expected, Ñandú had come begging to him after the successful search-and-destroy mission that had obliterated his base. He had arrived at the Octagon the morning after the raid pleading innocence of any wrongdoing and demanding an audience with Terra Nova.

"I never tried to rip you off," he'd insisted when they were in the privacy of Terra Nova's bug-proof office. "Why would I do such a thing? It is crazy!"

Ñandú's pockmarked face—with skin so resembling ostrich leather that the Spanish word for the large, flightless bird had become his handle—had been covered with sweat, which he'd constantly mopped with a handkerchief he clutched in his hand.

"One of my best men was killed," Terra Nova had stated coolly, eating salted cashew nuts from a bowl on his desk.

"It was not on my orders!" the frightened Ñandú had continued to insist as he'd squirmed in his seat. "By the Blessed Virgin, I tell you I had no part in this!" he'd asserted, frantically crossing himself.

"I believe you, my friend," Terra Nova had told Ñandú in a soothing voice, popping another handful of cashews into his mouth. "Now go, my brother. Your room is ready. Sit by the pool. Have a drink. After all, you are now my guest. *Mi casa es tu casa.*"

Terra Nova had watched the chastened dope runner close the door behind him while he munched another mouthful of cashews. A grim smile had twisted his face into an inhuman mask of hatred. Like the bird that was his namesake, Ñandú had been hiding his head in the sand by believing that the Mexican would allow him to live after his act of treachery.

Ñandú had done as Terra Nova had advised him. The pool had refreshed him, and he'd looked forward to enjoying a thirst-quenching champagne cocktail at one of the poolside tables when he'd finished his swim. However, that was not to be.

"What's going on?" Ñandú had shouted as two of Terra Nova's thugs grabbed hold of his arms the minute he'd come out of the pool.

They'd dragged the dripping, screaming drug dealer into the house, and Ñandú had realized then that Terra Nova had been toying with him all along, the way a cat toyed with a captive mouse.

It had already come to Terra Nova what he would do with Ñandú. While he had sat munching cashews and speaking soothingly to Ñandù, it had come to him.

As usual the inspiration was nothing short of ingenious. Terra Nova would throw a party on board his yacht in Tijuana Harbor, the *Choc Mool,* named after a Mayan rain god and bringer of good fortune. Ñandú would provide the entertainment, at least for Terra Nova.

Every few hours since the start of the party, days before, Terra Nova had taken a little more of Ñandú's life away from him. The doctor from Tijuana he had hired had assisted him in keeping the doomed man alive for as long as possible while Terra Nova made him pay for his transgression.

Now Terra Nova entered the ship's dispensary for another payback lick on his helpless enemy. The living corpse on the table already had one leg sliced off. The flesh of the other leg had been stripped completely away, exposing the raw, twitching bands of naked red musculature from beneath the thin covering of skin.

Ñandú's eyes bulged in terror and pain when he saw his tormentor. Adhesive tape covered his mouth so that he couldn't cry out, although with the loud music of the party on board the yacht, nobody would have heard him anyway.

"He is very weak," the doctor told Terra Nova as he called him aside. "He might not last."

"Give him something."

"I have shot him full of everything possible," the doctor answered, throwing up his arms in a gesture of desperation. "There is nothing more I can give him."

"All right," the Mexican doper assented, "whatever happens, happens." With the sound of a popular

American rap song thudding in the background from the sound system topside, Terra Nova picked up a surgical knife from a tray beside the table.

He inspected the gleaming blade of the precision cutting instrument under the glare of the light above the operating table in the yacht's dispensary.

Hardly aware that he was whistling the American tune, Terra Nova put the surgical scalpel's razor tip to Ñandú's throat and went to work.

OUTSIDE AGAIN, Terra Nova inhaled the invigorating salt air. His hundred-fifteen-foot yacht was anchored off the Acapulco shore. The party had been going full tilt for three days running, with guests shuttling to and from shore via motor launches provided by their host.

The noise of the party would assure that no one became aware of what was happening in the ship's dispensary. The presence of a number of important Mexican government officials would further guarantee that even if Terra Nova's secret was discovered, little or nothing would be done about it.

Slater, who had not been let in on the full scope of the payback scene, was also on board, discreetly watching his boss's back. Terra Nova had been very impressed by what Slater and his two commandos had been able to accomplish on the night raid against Ñandú's Tapachula drug factory.

So pleased was he, in fact, that he had another job already lined up for the three of them.

While the guests on board the *Choc Mool* partied around the clock, Hawke and Bishop were farther north, across the border in California, scouting out a strike on an armory full of advanced weapons. Terra Nova had called them into his inner sanctum at the Octagon and informed them that he had already bribed base personnel, who had guaranteed they could plunder a warehouse building with impunity.

Hawke and Bishop were ordered to check out the situation before Terra Nova would sanction the raid on the armory. They would have to make sure that the soldier who had been bought off to unlock the arms warehouse doors was legit.

The raid would be carried out quietly. It would be low-profile or it wouldn't go down at all.

"Slater, come here," Terra Nova called to his security chief when he ran into him topside. When Slater came over, Terra Nova introduced him to a man of early middle age. The first thing he noticed about the man was his eyes. Crazy eyes. The same kind of eyes that Terra Nova possessed.

"This is a man I want you to meet," he said to Slater. "I have told him much about you. Deal Slater, please shake hands with my Colombian colleague, Rogelio la Carne."

Slater played it cool and hoped the shock of the sudden encounter didn't register on his face. The Colombian had been seldom photographed, and the grainy surveillance photos he'd studied prior to the mission were not much like the drug baron in the flesh. Carne's pale gray eyes were locked on his as though they were living lie detectors.

Slater had encountered the same kind of stare many times before. There were those who believed that their eyes possessed the superhuman ability to detect all untruth, all deception. Carne had the eyes of such men.

"Mr. Slater," Carne declared, "I have heard of your exploits. Come. Let us talk."

The three of them went into Terra Nova's private cabin. They sat in comfortable chairs of Italian leather as Terra Nova passed around joints and a bag of snort. While the druglords partook of the reefer and coke, Slater abstained.

"Mr. Slater is a teetotaler," Terra Nova said as he snorted cocaine off the mirror surface of the low table between them. "I suppose a man in his profession must be."

"Of course," Carne acknowledged. "Which brings me to a question. I know that Francisco has told you something of our larger goals. I am in need of borrowing your services to train my people," he explained.

"That's up to Mr. Terra Nova," Slater replied.

"Then it's settled," Terra Nova returned. "I want you to go to Colombia. That is, if the arms shipment is a go. Rogelio must have a trained body of men soon. Take both of your partners with you."

"Okay by me," Slater said.

Just then the phone rang. Terra Nova picked it up and spoke a few words in Spanish into the handset, then switched to English.

"Splendid, splendid!" Slater heard him say. "Tomorrow night, then. Right. I'll tell him."

Terra Nova cradled the handset.

"That was your two colleagues," he said to Slater. "Everything checked out. The armory raid is a go."

15

The sentry's face wore a frightened expression as he emerged from the guard post and trundled open the main gate on heavy rollers. It was the expression of a man who has suddenly realized that he might have gotten himself into something way over his head.

For a moment his eyes locked with those of the hard-looking man in crisp ODs sitting behind the steering wheel of the military two-and-a-half-ton truck waiting at the gate.

That one look was enough to make the soldier squirm. Despite the warm California air, a cold chill ran down his spine. Without knowing why, his right hand automatically rose to his head and he began a smart salute.

The heavy vehicle rolled past the sentry into the compound encircled by the twenty-foot-high security fence before he could complete his salute to the man with military bearing sitting behind the wheel.

As he watched the red taillights wink off when the truck rounded a corner, the sentry's pulse rate skyrocketed, and he was thankful there was nobody around to notice the new sweat beading his face.

ELAPSED MISSION TIME: five minutes.

The cache of weapons and ordnance was located in a hangarlike structure identified only as Terminal F.

The deuce-and-a-half with Slater behind the wheel and Bishop and Hawke riding in the canvas-covered rear crossed the temporarily unguarded compound without a hitch.

Reaching the warehouse terminal building, Slater backed the truck into the loading dock, which was unlocked and unguarded. Then he, Hawke and Bishop hustled out of the transport and into the warehouse.

The grunt they'd paid off promised that he could guarantee the raiders twenty minutes of foraging time, and they would have to shake their tail feathers to make it back out again by the deadline.

Inside the arms depot, Slater and company quickly found the weapons. They were stacked in labeled, modularized transportation and storage cases that rose to the ceiling.

Protected-reach forklift trucks were conveniently parked nearby, and the trio used these to quickly and efficiently haul the stolen arms over to the transport truck, where Bishop loaded each successive skid of matériel onto the truck.

By the time their twenty-minute deadline was up, Slater, Hawke and Bishop had grabbed enough small arms and explosives to equip a small army. Sliding behind the wheel of the truck again, Slater shifted into gear and rolled back to the sentry box by the gate.

The GI who had been bribed to allow the heist crew egress to the base was small change compared to the targets heading SLAM's hit list.

Nevertheless, he had dishonored his country by selling out to corrupt manipulators like Terra Nova. SLAM had already made damn sure that the GI would be cooling his heels in the base stockade before long. Those who swam with the sharks and were not sharks themselves would wind up shark food.

As for the stolen weapons, they wouldn't benefit the drug cartel one single bit. The guns and ordnance removed during the night's raid would only serve as bait to entice the narcotraffickers toward their final reckoning.

"Hope you got what you wanted," the sentry said, summoning his courage as the deuce-and-a-half rolled away from the gate into the night. Yes, they did, thought Slater. And soon enough, the sentry would get exactly what he deserved.

PART TWO:
THE HAMMER AND THE ANVIL

16

The convoy of two-and-a-half-ton trucks laden with weapons, food and supplies churned up the muddy mountain road. Rain fell in dense, twisting torrents through the two-tiered jungle canopy.

Porting Ultimax machine guns kept dry beneath the rubberized canvas slickers they wore, Slater, Hawke and Bishop rode shotgun over the convoy.

As powerful as Carne was in this part of the world, there were guerrilla bands and hostile *Indios* traversing the region who didn't care diddly about whose path they crossed or whose toes they stepped on. They could and did stage ambushes without giving thought to the consequences of retribution from Carne or, for that matter, anybody else.

The Indian who was their guide soon indicated to the gringo mercenaries that they had nearly reached the site of the enormous cocaine-processing plant that Carne had spent the past two years carving out of the virgin jungle.

The coke factory, which Carne had code-named Finca El Rábano, or the Radish Farm, was located in the Colombian south, an area isolated from the rest of the country by dense rain forest and an extensive river system, far from his lavish estate in the mountain region farther north.

Carne fancied himself the Spanish country gentleman. His sprawling ranch was his refuge against the often violent realities of the brutal line of business he was engaged in.

In the hacienda's cool, airy spaces la Carne could breed his prize Thoroughbred Paso Fino stallions and play golf on his private links. There, too, he could entertain prestigious guests from all over the world and dream of an empire he would one day build, an empire stretching from one end of South America to the other.

It was at Finca El Rábano where things got down to the nitty-gritty, where the raw materials from which Carne would build his criminal empire were forged into weapons of power. In the humid depths of the jungle the cocaine godfather had assembled a group of hardmen, *pistolas* and mercs drawn from the international talent pool, who had signed on to fill the ranks of Carne's private army.

But the mercenary force that Carne was trying to cobble together was still an untrained and untested assortment of motley killers, petty thieves and social misfits.

Mean but still green, it needed not only the weapons that were being brought in by truck but also the combat-honed skills of professional soldiers to weld it into the kind of crack paramilitary shock force that would give Carne the muscle required to translate his dreams of grandeur into realities of conquest.

That was to be the task of the three American mercenaries whom Carne had gotten on loan from his Mexican connection, Francisco Terra Nova. The South American drug honcho was counting on Slater, Hawke and Bishop to build him a fighting force that could give him a stranglehold on Colombian politics.

"The government in Bogotá is weak and soft," Carne had explained to Slater. "They are cowards who no longer have the balls to fight. All it will take is the proper amount of force applied correctly to topple it forever."

The coup d'état planned by Carne would make him the unchallenged master of the country. Soon the region would belong to him, as well.

By 0900 hours, as a cold, stinging mist blew low across the muddy land, the convoy crested a final hill and rolled down into the verdant, low-lying region that made up the five-square-mile facility that was their destination. Slater, Hawke and Bishop were impressed by the size and sophistication of the encampment.

This was no second-rate operation like Ñandú's slipshod drug factory on the Guatemalan coast. Carne had set up shop with all the extras here.

The plant was a true monster. The central facility was a hangar-size inflatable all-weather hut, with a central air-conditioning system and a helipad nearby.

There was an elaborate system of conveyor belts designed for hauling the raw coca plants from the docks along the muddy river that meandered past the plant and from the airfield where scores of DC-4 planeloads per day could be flown in from Peru and other regional supply centers.

As the trucks rolled into the installation, they were challenged at the main gate by a guard in jungle pattern BDUs armed with a Valmet autorifle. The guard was one of the foreign mercs on Carne's payroll, and Slater took note of the fact that these free-lancers made up the perimeter security force instead of the usual crew of vicious but unprofessional *pistolas*.

Two security crow's nests perched atop thirty-foot-high towers watched over the compound. Each was equipped by a searchlight beacon and a .50-caliber machine gun, and was well sited for both perimeter surveillance and defense.

The facility was strategically positioned, too. One side abutted the muddy river, which ran north and south, while a twenty-foot security apron of bare land cleared from jungle prevented an attacking force from sneaking up undetected.

The armed merc at the gate checked out the newcomers and waved them through. The man was hard faced and all business. He was a blue-eyed, crew-cut Anglo who talked with an Aussie accent, and he had the look of a jungle veteran. Probably he'd been a player in the proxy wars of the region that had been waged throughout the eighties.

Slater, Hawke and Bishop supervised the unloading of the stolen weapons and combat matériel. Again Carne had equipped the jungle base with state-of-the-art facilities for warehousing the illicitly obtained assortment of high-tech small arms and sophisticated ordnance.

The Quonset hut storage area was a good sixty feet long by twenty feet wide. It was outfitted with gun racks, pallets for stacking ordnance, modularized boxes for ammunition storage and protected-reach forklift vehicles for moving the stuff around for distribution to personnel or transloading to trucks.

The warehouse was also centrally air-conditioned to keep the ammunition from cooking off in the often intense jungle heat, and the humidity from corroding the metal of the guns and nonplastic munitions casings.

Slater was coming out of the warehouse after seeing to the cachement of the arms when a man wearing paramilitary cammies walked over to him and extended his hand. He introduced himself as Gordon Ryecroft, and he said he was El Caudillo, the leader of mercenary forces for the jungle facility. Slater had been expecting him.

"Heard quite a bit about you, mate," the merc told Slater in an Aussie accent. "Not just now that you've been operating free-lance, but before, too. In Nicaragua, Afghanistan, then Iraq."

"Glad to meet you," Slater answered, shaking hands and noting the look of suspicion in Ryecroft's washed-out blue eyes set in a lean-jowled, cadaverous face that resembled a living skull. The merc wasn't making small talk when he let Slater know that he'd heard of him, he realized right off. Ryecroft was wondering aloud what a guy with his career credentials was doing on his own hook.

He was telling Slater that he didn't trust him, that he would be keeping his eyes on him.

It wouldn't be the first time, though, that a top-notch fighting man had been mistreated by the U.S. military. As a general rule Delta and American Special Forces ate their own. Slater could have refused to eat

one ration of shit too many or stepped on the wrong
toes. Which might—accent on *might*—explain what he
was doing boondocking around as a free-lance operative.

"Let me show you around, mate," Ryecroft told
Slater. "Damn proud of this little operation," he continued as they arrived at the first stop on his tour.
"This is our main processing lab. Every aspect of the
process is computer controlled. To make sure that the
product is high quality, we even have a resident chemist. Hey, doc, come over here a minute."

Slater saw the tall, weedy-looking man in checked
cowboy shirt, worn blue jeans and wire-frame glasses
look up from a table cluttered with technical gear, then
get up and and head their way. The guy was the book-
worm type, with lank, unkempt blond hair, the kind
central casting would use to play a mad scientist in a
horror flick.

"Heinz Kladen, meet Deal Slater. Kladen was a right
high-ranking tech expert in the East German government's Intelligence ministry," Ryecroft went on with a
smile, and Slater saw Kladen squirm. Ryecroft was
obviously enjoying it. "Yeah, Kladen had to leave the
old DDR in quite a hurry. It seems he was accused of
torturing people for the infamous Stasi, ain't that right,
mate?"

The scientist made a feeble attempt at a smile. "These rumors were all untrue," he protested. "I never worked for the Stasi. Please, Ryecroft, I have asked you not to carry on this way."

"Yeah, you're right, doc," Ryecroft said, still smiling. "You were only following orders, right? I forgot you *Deutschland über Alles* types always stick to the party line."

Kladen stood there nonplussed, at a loss for a reply, and Ryecroft, wearing a smirk, sent him back to his labors.

Ryecroft ushered Slater out of the lab after explaining more about how the coke-refinement process worked here at the Radish Farm. Then he showed Slater the bunkhouses, the camp training grounds, the dispensary, the transport facilities and one of the base's two canteens—one of which was off-limits to the rank and file.

Finally he showed Slater to his own billet. The accommodations were well equipped, with a ceramic flush toilet and hot and cold running water and a small refrigerator unit. They were air-conditioned, too, and even had satellite TV. All the comforts of a first-class hotel, thought Slater as Ryecroft left him, if you didn't mind the view. As he cracked the fridge and found a liter bottle of mineral water inside it, Slater almost regretted having to blow the place to hell.

17

Two sentries stood by the guardhouse at the main gate. They looked and acted bored.

One merc slouched on the ledge of the open guardhouse window, his rifle nowhere in sight.

The other sentry sat on a plastic milk crate and smoked a cigarette, his Valmet assault weapon lying on the ground near his feet. Obviously these two men believed they had good reason to expect that nothing too heavy would go down anytime soon.

Walking across the compound, Slater approached the two mercs. They had been introduced earlier to the new top kick by Ryecroft and were both aware of who he was. They also knew that Slater wielded a lot of clout with Carne and was in a position to give them orders.

"How's it going?" Slater casually asked the freelance talent.

"Pretty good," one of the two sentries answered, although neither made any effort to assume a more soldierly appearance, "if you don't mind the damn mosquitoes."

"Or the bloody dysentery," the other guy chimed in.

"Yeah, right," the first merc affirmed. "That, too."

It was a hot night and the mosquitos were indeed out with a vengeance. Bitten by one, the first guard who had spoken slapped at his neck and cursed the troublesome insects.

"Okay," Slater returned. "Catch you guys later."

Taped to his leg, a receiver unit sensitive to infrared radiation had just triggered a tactile feedback pad in contact with Slater's skin. The soundless vibratory signal came as a result of the markings on the black special-issue combat dress worn by Hawke and Bishop, which emitted IR radiation, the extension of a technique developed in Operation Desert Storm.

Though he hadn't seen them, Slater knew that the two black-suited shadows had just slid through a cut-out section of security perimeter fence nearby and had slipped from the camp compound into the outlying forest. Slater had distracted the guards long enough to ensure that Hawke and Bishop extracted from the base perimeter without incident.

There was to be a drop of a sophisticated piece of special demolition ordnance within the next hour. Specifically the ordnance was a SADM, a special atomic demolition munition.

The low-yield subkiloton tactical nuclear device was capable of generating enough destructive power to raze the entire coke-processing operation to the ground.

Only a smoldering depression would remain where the camp had formerly stood. The modest radioactivity levels produced by the SADM would be manageable, and the U.S. Atomic Energy Commission would immediately contact the Colombian government with a generous offer to send cleanup teams into the area to decontaminate it. The Colombians would have no choice but to agree to an offer they couldn't refuse.

True, deploying the SADM would be playing dirty with the Colombian government, hitting them below the belt. But turnabout was fair play.

SLAM hadn't been created to negotiate with the drug producers, packagers and distributors who had been playing just as dirty with U.S. citizens. It had been mandated at the highest level, by direct Presidential finding, to go out and do what no other executive or law-enforcement agency had yet been able to accomplish in the prosecution of America's war on drugs— cut through the bullshit and solidly nail the elusive shadow figures at the source of the drug supply line.

Niceties of international law, diplomatic concern for stepping on the toes of America's allies, claims and counterclaims from all sides to the contrary, it was on American streets that the Colombian narcobarons peddled their wares of death, American users who were hooked on the poison they pushed.

In the end it would be Americans who had to act for themselves and on their own as they had done historically to eradicate evils that had plagued their nation.

HAWKE AND BISHOP located the clandestine drop zone using a hand-held Magellan NAV 1000M GPS for precision land navigation. The DZ was a jungle clearing where spear grass had taken root amid the remnants of lightning-scorched trees. If events proceeded according to schedule, the light single-engine plane flying down from Panama would circle and paradrop the SADM.

Its position updated by constant satellite telemetry, the Magellan GPS unit brought them to their destination without a hitch. Reaching the DZ, Bishop unshipped the hand-held tactical communications beacon, flipped up the transponder's compact yet wide-ranging antenna and energized the unit.

The red status light and LCD panel showed that the signal was being transmitted on a VHF 243 MHz bandwidth and that its lithium battery was operating at maximum efficiency.

The drop aircraft would home in on the transponder's radio beacon by means of a dedicated two-channel-sensitive homer pod mounted on its nose assembly, and would thus precisely locate their position.

The two-man team settled down to wait. It was 0340 hours and the light plane, a Piper Cub, was expected at precisely 0400 hours.

After a couple of minutes of waiting for the drop, Hawke and Bishop heard the plane's approach in the form of a muted droning sound from the north. Soon they could make out the profile of the aircraft swooping in low across the tree line.

Instead of circling in a reconnaissance pass as it was scheduled to, the Cub kept on going until it passed directly overhead and disappeared over the tree line. Hawke and Bishop heard the telltale spluttering of an engine experiencing serious problems. Minutes later the din of a crash came echoing through the forest.

"What the hell do you make of that?" Hawke asked Bishop.

"Only one way we're gonna know," he returned. "Let's check it out."

They set off in the direction that the aircraft's unstable flight path had taken it. It was a mile or so of rough going through dense jungle underbrush before they were finally able to locate the crash site.

The wreckage of the Piper Cub was lying nose down in a quicksand bog. The fuselage of the light plane was almost completely submerged in the brackish waters and sinking fast.

Hawke and Bishop had no way of retrieving the SADM on board in the minutes remaining before the aircraft vanished entirely. As they debated their next course of action, they heard a moaning sound coming from nearby. When they investigated they discovered the Cub's pilot.

He'd been thrown clear of the cockpit when the plane had crashed but was badly busted up. Hawke looked at Bishop and shook his head. He didn't need a medical degree to be damn sure that the pilot was a goner.

"Engine...went out," the pilot wheezed, coughing up a bloody discharge. "Couldn't...hold her steady." He feebly clutched at Hawke's arms, then shivered all over. His back arched and then, his struggle ended, went finally limp.

By this time the plane had completely vanished from view beneath the murky waters of the bog. In the interests of operational secrecy, the pilot would have to go the same way.

Hawke and Bishop carried the pilot's slack, broken body over to the edge of the bog and laid him gently in the quicksand. The bog began to do its work and sucked the body down. In minutes both the pilot and the plane he'd flown in had vanished forever.

SLATER WAS WONDERING what was holding up his two men. Hawke and Bishop should have returned to the encampment long before. Slater had gone back to the guard booth by 0430 hours, ready to distract the sentries' attention again while Hawke and Bishop slipped back through the perimeter fence.

The two men had been out-of-bounds a lot longer than scheduled, and Slater knew they'd hit a glitch somewhere along the line. He was debating what, if anything, he could do about the situation when the concealed signal unit taped to his calf registered the strobe of Hawke and Bishop's IR-radiating garment patches.

Back in his quarters after Hawke and Bishop had stolen into camp once again, Slater conferred with his two commando teammates. Hawke and Bishop briefed him about the events at the drop zone. Slater carefully considered the team's remaining options for a couple of minutes. He finally decided that there was no way SLAM was going to walk away from this operation without giving it the old school try.

18

It was twenty minutes until sunrise at 0516 hours. Slater, Bishop and Hawke cammied up, checked their gear and shifted into overdrive.

Now, without being able to deploy the SADM that had been lost in the bungled airdrop, they would have to find another method to reduce Carne's jungle dope factory to a mass of smoldering wreckage.

Fortunately the huge cache of arms and munitions that Carne himself had stockpiled in anticipation of his takeover of the Colombian government was a ready-made source of weapons and explosives.

SLAM's first step toward putting the mission back on track would be to stage a hit-and-git raid on the narcobaron's private armory. There they would be able to lay hands on enough ordnance to wire the installation to blow sky-high and commandeer enough firepower to fight their way out of the base if the going started getting tough.

SLATER STRODE up to the sentry stationed outside the armory's main entranceway, which was covered by a big roll-down gate of cantilevered steel. Set farther along the wall was a smaller steel door, an entrance for personnel use.

"How's it hanging, pal?" Slater asked the guard, one merc to another. The sentry knew who Slater was and figured he was conducting a surprise inspection.

The sentry shifted his M-16 in his arms and began to say something in broken English with a thick French accent. But before he could get the sentence out of his mouth, Slater rammed his bunched left fist into the sentry's stomach and used the flat of his right hand to deliver a savage blow to the septum, which sent jagged cartilage into the frontal lobes of his brain.

The merc immediately went limp and folded up in a heap on the ground. Within seconds Hawke had produced burglar tools and picked the lock on the side door quickly and soundlessly. Hawke scooted inside with Bishop two steps behind him.

Slater dragged the dead sentry inside the arms dump via the same route used by his crew. In the few seconds that Slater had required to take down the watchman, his two SLAM teammates had already dispatched the rest of the mercs inside who were guarding Carne's cache of combat matériel.

Struck in the vitals by whispering parabellums shot from silenced SMGs, the mercs were easily dealt with. All that was left to do was stash the bodies and get on with the arms shopping.

Thanks to the professional inventory-management system that Carne used, it was a relatively simple matter to locate all the matériel they required to blow the Radish Farm straight to hell, and then some.

The compact automatic weapons ported by Hawke and Bishop were slung over their shoulders, and armament designed for heavier duty drawn from stocks. Bishop selected a lightweight M-60E3 Maremont machine gun equipped with a 100-round box mag of 7.62 mm steeljackets.

The Ultimax machine guns ported by the team when they had arrived at the base were world-class weapons. But nothing matched the stopping power of NATO-caliber 7.62 x 51 mm bullets as far as Bishop was concerned. Spare ammo mags were socked away in musette bags slung at his waist for quick magazine changes.

Slater also armed himself with an M-60E3. SLAM's combat-seasoned leader was convinced from long experience that the lightweight carbine version of the original Vietnam-era M-60 packed the heavy-duty punch he needed on a mission where he faced long odds and was outgunned.

Hawke was also interested in all the stopping power he could get his hands on. But for SLAM's junior member the Ultimax's light weight, high magazine capacity and operating flexibility more than made up for any deficiencies of the 5.56 mm cartridges it fired.

Along with Hawke and Bishop, Slater outfitted himself with an assortment of grenades of various configurations, which he slung from load-bearing suspenders around his BDUs. The black night-action garb used in the abortive SADM drop wouldn't be suited to operations in the mixed light and shadow conditions of the coming early-morning twilight.

Now equipped with a formidable mix of lethal small arms, the SLAM crew proceeded to check out the ordnance available to blow the base. They were gratified to discover that Carne's arms dump was as well stocked with these items as it was with small arms and ammo.

The job was doable.

The shaped demolition charges were available in an assortment of configurations from prismatic to concave. They loaded up on as many as they could carry and completed their dog-robbing spree by wiring the arms dump to shoot the moon with the last charges they'd boosted.

Within minutes after they had broken into the arms depot, the three commandos had all the gear they would require to send the mammoth drug-processing facility fireballing up into the wild black yonder.

EACH MEMBER of the three-man blitz detail had selected then deployed to several operational sites. Before they had separated, Slater had given Bishop and Hawke the team's rendezvous point.

They were to mine the camp and haul ass before 0615 hours to one of the small storage sheds located near the motor pool area. SLAM's dominant strategy was to grab some transport, disable all other vehicles and bust out just before the charges went ballistic.

Mason Hawke's target was the barracks unit, Bishop's main objective was the radio shack, as it was vital that communications lines be severed when the demo charges blew, while Slater's primary target was the central processing facility itself.

GORDON RYECROFT, the Radish Farm's top merc, was a chronic insomniac. Years of living on the edge had made sleep a condition to be dreaded rather than enjoyed, a source of fear rather than replenishment. He popped uppers to make sure that he stayed awake at all times.

Ryecroft had learned long ago that, when asleep, a man was at his most vulnerable. In his line of work it could be downright dangerous to one's health. The merc especially hated the quiet hours just preceding dawn—hours that were best suited to the launching of surprise attacks.

It was during those dangerous hours that Ryecroft liked to walk about the camp compound, keeping an eye on Carne's investment and his own source of livelihood.

Ryecroft shrugged on a pair of well-worn BDUs and took leave of his billet. He walked slowly, sweating in the high humidity and listening to bullfrogs croaking from the river beyond the trees. Though he'd lived in jungle environments half his life, Ryecroft still hadn't gotten completely used to the sights, sounds, smells and feel of such places.

Hardly had Ryecroft progressed two hundred feet into the compound and reached the area between his quarters and the motor pool when the veteran mercenary sensed that something was awry.

He stood stock-still. The weird feeling that somewhere, somehow, stuff was hitting the fan was overpowering. Alarm bells were going off in his head. One other thing long experience in the field had taught Ryecroft was that a merc's best friend was his own instinct for survival.

Keeping his eyes wide open and his senses on full alert, Ryecroft started walking again. When he reached the armory, he noticed that the sentry posted at its entrance was no longer on duty. His suspicions of trouble were confirmed, but Ryecroft knew better than to sing out for help.

All that would accomplish would be to give away his position and set him up for a fast takedown from a shooter crouched in the shadows. Instead, he drew a SIG P-228 semiauto from the hip holster riding his garrison belt, cocked the piece out of long habit although it was double-action and stepped cautiously into the arms dump.

Ryecroft found the dead sentry wedged behind some munitions stack boxes. Crouching down on the balls of his feet, he touched two fingertips to the sentry's throat. The body was still warm, and rigor mortis hadn't yet completely set in.

Ryecroft realized that the sentry had to have been dusted only minutes before his arrival. A single thought flashed through his mind.

Deal Slater. It had to be him.

Ryecroft's instincts had warned him from the very first that there was something definitely not legitimate about Slater. For one thing, a man like him didn't ever go free-lance.

Slater was government issue. Like a rifle or a hand grenade or a Stealth fighter. Guys like Slater either retired feetfirst or with a pension. Never did they turn solo—not unless their solo act was a cover for something else, of course.

A few minutes of searching the armory clearly demonstrated to Ryecroft that several deadly items of armament were missing from the weapons stores of the dump, though his hasty search hadn't turned up the hidden demo charges.

Knowing there was no time to waste, Ryecroft made tracks from the depot and hustled across the base compound. Raising holy hell and having the men scour the perimeter was his first thought, but in the end Ryecroft decided to take care of business another way.

He was going to take out Slater personally. It would score him big points with his benefactor, Carne. In certain circles it might even make him a kind of a celebrity.

19

The logistics of taking down the Radish Farm were different from those SLAM had dealt with at Ñandú's coke refinery.

But the principle of cooking raw coca down to cocaine base—and ultimately crystalline powder—was essentially the same anywhere the art was practiced.

The process hinged on an all-important central component, as necessary to the finished product as the coca leaves themselves: highly volatile ethyl ether had to be used in large quantities.

There were enough fifty-five-gallon drums of the inflammable solvent stored at the installation to send the entire facility rocketing moonward. All that was necessary was a little encouragement, and all it would take was the right push in the right places.

A hard SLAM where it counted most.

Slater night-walked across the coke-processing center, slotting his shaped demo charges where they'd do the greatest damage. The second of his two musettes soon was empty, and Slater was ready to call it quits when he suddenly heard a familiar voice behind him.

"Turn around slowly, mate," Ryecroft commanded. "Let's see those hands raised high."

Slater did as ordered. He found himself staring at Ryecroft, who wore a lopsided grin on his cadaverous face.

"Disarm those charges, boyo, and right quick, too," Ryecroft ordered after he'd stripped Slater of his weapons. "Don't try to fuck me, Slater. I could bloody well kill you now and disarm them myself."

"Sure," Slater acknowledged to the gun-wielding merc. "Anything you say, Ryecroft."

Slater deactivated the HE charges by changing the detonation time that he'd programmed into their memory chips to zero hours. Ryecroft watched him like a hawk until he was assured that the charges were in fact neutralized.

After a few minutes of checking out the installation and satisfying himself that all the bombs had really been deactivated, he frog-marched his American captive out into the slowly fading twilight at the point of his SIG 9 mm pistol.

"We'll just take ourselves a little stroll," Ryecroft said almost pleasantly, picking up Slater's M-60E3. "Find your other two mates. You know where they are, of course. Lead me to them if you're smart."

Slater brought Ryecroft on toward his own billet, the single place where neither Hawke nor Bishop was supposed to be, but that either might pass on his way to the team's rally point.

At that moment, having completed his placement of explosives, Hawke was hustling toward the motor pool RV chosen to stage the team's bust-out bid when he spotted Slater with Ryecroft's gun jammed into his kidneys.

Unfortunately Ryecroft had also spotted Hawke. Tensed for trouble, Ryecroft had the drop on Hawke as he pivoted to snap off a couple of 9 mm slugs at the SLAM commando. Ryecroft's split-second advantage meant that Hawke, who was bringing up his Ultimax a hair too slowly, would end up the odd man out.

Slater moved at the same moment that Ryecroft turned aside. An upward-sweeping hard block upset Ryecroft's aim, and the SIG fired a round harmlessly into the air.

Hawke cut loose with an autoburst of Ultimax 5.56 mm steel, but Ryecroft was already booking for cover, having dropped the machine gun taken from Slater during the process of escape. The Australian was fast and he knew when the odds weren't in his favor anymore.

Ryecroft now began firing his pistol at the sky, counting on the sound of gunshots to awaken the slumbering men in the bunkhouses and the mercs in the watchtowers and send all into action. He'd have preferred to punch Slater's ticket on his own hook, but if he had to share the glory for taking him down, then so be it. Better than dying.

Spotlights from the guard towers now lanced downward toward the source of the sudden gunfire. From the barracks the shouts of rudely awakened mercs clashed with the frightened barking of camp dogs as lights flicked on and faces were silhouetted against windows.

Carne's forces were already spilling into the night moments later, pulling on clothes and brandishing weapons as they milled around, searching for the enemy.

Then a deafening explosion sledgehammered through the jungle, resounding in the predawn murk. The earth shook fiercely as the violent blast effect bowled over tall trees growing on the base perimeter and sent them crashing to the ground.

In the next heartbeat the charges that Bishop had planted at the radio shack went off, too, and talons of hellfire clawed at the sky. Cocooned in flames, the radio mast keeled sideways then toppled onto the roof of the shack with a deafening boom.

"Come on!" Slater shouted to Hawke over the thunder of the detonating munitions and the chaotic pulses of sporadic gunfire that had begun to crackle through the compound as ammo supplies cooked off. "The main refinery shack has got to be taken down. Otherwise we came a long way to do nothing at all."

Now the mercs were sighting in on Slater and Hawke. Slater grabbed up the M-60E3 he'd retrieved from Ryecroft.

The strike zone had turned white-hot. SLAM was on a fast train. Positioning themselves back-to-back, Slater and Hawke got set to clean house.

Whipsawing 7.62 mm rivets flailed from the wailing M-60 at Slater's hip, chopping down the charging mercs who were heaving steel on a flat-out run.

Hawke's hardware was bucking in his fists, too. Glowing tracer rounds zigzagged through the night as the Ultimax cycled out its annihilating firestream, ripping into human flesh and butchering everything that it touched.

The combined effect of the two jackhammering autoweapons was pure, bloody mayhem.

Their bodies jerking and shuddering as they became grotesquely animated under a pounding wave of high-velocity bursts, Carne's mercs flung their arms into the air, firing autobursts skyward before they dropped to the dirt.

It didn't take long for the auto-heat firestorm to punch out an escape corridor for the two SLAM commandos.

Bolting through it, Slater and Hawke soon reached the central processing shack where Slater had been intercepted by Ryecroft not a half hour before.

Slater had no time to rearm all the prismatic charges he'd planted there. The place had to blow *now,* or the way the battle was shaping, it wouldn't blow at all. Moving fast while Hawke covered him with the Ultimax, Slater set as many of the charges as he could for a four-minute delay, then both he and Hawke booked for cover as fast as their pumping legs could carry them.

A tremendous roaring filled the air. Massive shock waves radiating outward from the epicenter of the explosion hurled both SLAM commandos to the ground though they were dozens of yards away from the demo site by then.

The intensity of the blast was so powerful that mercs caught near ground zero were instantly blown to smithereens, and sundered body parts were sent mushrooming in all directions by the explosion's concussive effect.

Human torches reeled crazily through the death and thunder of the convulsing lunatic night. The screams of maimed and bleeding men mingled with the maddening din of secondary explosions as fuel drums ignited and munitions stores cooked off.

"Hook up with Bishop at the rally point," Slater shouted at Hawke above the hellish uproar of multiple detonations. "I'm going after Ryecroft."

HEINZ KLADEN STAGGERED from the kitchen and dropped the chicken leg he'd been chewing on, and watched with a stunned expression as cooked-off LAW rockets shot up into the night. A few moments later he saw the refinery hut blown skyward.

The German chemist was billeted in a small room at the hut's rear, right by the laboratory where he worked. The German realized that if not for his hunger pangs, he would undoubtedly have been reduced to a handful of smoldering ashes by now.

Kladen was no fool. He knew that his time here in the jungle was up. It was no surprise. He'd seen it coming for a long time now.

But he'd taken precautions. The funds he'd deposited from his earnings into a numbered Swiss bank account were sufficient to pay for several years of easy living in the playgrounds of Europe. He'd made his pile. If he could just pull his fat out of the fire in one piece, all he'd have to worry about was how to spend it.

Kladen had also set up contingency plans for escape. Road, river and air routes were all mapped out in his head. Today the chemist was doubly lucky.

First and foremost, he was still kicking. Secondly he knew the Beech Duke used in a recent supply run still sat on the jungle airstrip, ready for takeoff. He was an excellent pilot and would have no difficulty in flying the plane to safety.

Kladen dodged through the crackling flames and cascading shrapnel toward the runway. He ran into two mercs in a pickup whom he sometimes paid to do odd jobs for him and occasionally scout for the choicer women in nearby towns to warm his lonely bed.

The meeting was another stroke of good luck for Kladen. Hans and Erich were both native Berliners like himself and would come in mighty handy as bodyguards.

"Get me to the airstrip," he said to them in German after flagging them down. "We take the plane together."

Hans and Erich both readily agreed. Kladen jumped into the truck's cargo area while Hans wrenched the steering wheel, pointed the truck toward the runway and stomped on the pedal.

20

Slater picked up Ryecroft's trail at the big muddy river that flowed past the camp. Ryecroft had one foot on the dock and the other aboard one of the two Flairboots used by the installation to transport personnel and supplies up- and downriver.

Carne's German-designed surface-effect boats were faster than any conventional river craft. They rode on a cushion of air by a process known as "flairing"— low-level airfoil-generated flight—and were not fazed in the least by any but the largest obstacles. An obstacle such as a small island was no problem for a Flairboot. It would simply fly across it.

Slater unleashed an M-60E3 burst as the Flairboot sped away, but Ryecroft was already considerably out of range by the time he could bring the gun into play. Slater hustled up to the dock and got on board the other surface-effect craft, untied its hawser lines and revved up the engine.

The flying boat's powerful rear- and under-mounted fans threw up mighty gusts of wind, and Slater was off and running seconds later in hot pursuit at speeds nearing one hundred fifty miles per hour. By now the indigo sky of early morning was already beginning to turn pink around the edges, and full daylight was only a matter of minutes away.

In the catbird seat at the rear of the stub-winged craft, Ryecroft looked back and saw the second Flairboot eating up the water behind him. He reached between his legs and grabbed the AUG assault weapon that he'd placed beside him in case he ran into trouble.

Lightweight and lethal, Steyr's Army Universal Gun was stable enough to be fired one-handed. This was an important consideration, given the merc's present need to crank out accurate fire from the juddering deck of a fast-moving boat.

As the channel widened into a broad swath of muddy river flow, Ryecroft half turned in his seat and cut loose with a long burst of 5.56 mm tumblers at the pursuing Flairboot while keeping his other hand tight on the throttle.

Slater skewed his own Flairboot hard to the left, barely evading the incoming fusillade. He raised the over-under M-16A2/M-203 combo he'd grabbed as a backup before taking off after Ryecroft and calculated the windage and trajectory needed to hit the target with a grenade round. A 40 mm can was already loaded into the bloop tube.

A trigger pull sent the grenade round bursting into the air with a loud whup, and the launcher bucked in the SLAM honcho's fist. Slater's aim was good, though not especially accurate.

The shell landed short of the fast-moving Flairboot, yards to port. Slater quickly loaded another HE round into the under-mounted grenade launcher and let Ryecroft have another one.

He'd taped the merc better this time, and the shell exploded much closer to the speeding target craft. But although the burst doused Ryecroft with silty river water and clumps of uprooted duckweed, it still didn't slow him down any.

Ryecroft fired off another burst, then whipped the Flairboot into one of the narrow estuary channels feeding off the river's main trunk.

Having gone around the bend of an island, he was momentarily out of Slater's line of sight. The weed-choked backwater region was a maze of small islands overgrown with dense mangrove jungle separated by narrow, muddy channels.

Slater rounded the bend in the river a moment later. Finding Ryecroft gone, he slowed almost to a dead stop as he approached the first of several inlets.

Ryecroft wasn't dumb, Slater knew. He could be waiting just beyond the inlet mouth with the AUG, ready to let him have it with a put-away burst.

Edging up carefully, Slater saw that the channel was empty.

Damn! he thought.

Ryecroft had gotten clean away.

In the bewildering maze of channels he might lose Slater entirely, and it was a sure bet that Ryecroft, who'd been at the facility for months, knew the area well.

Despite the fact that Ryecroft had expertly maneuvered Slater into a trap, Slater had no choice but to press on in pursuit. Besides the destruction of the mammoth coke factory, SLAM's mission called for putting Carne away permanently.

With the narcobaron still in business, it would only be a matter of time before another Radish Farm sprang up somewhere else and the coke started flowing again in quantities more massive than before, a river of high-grade snort that would wash its poison onto the streets of American cities.

Shifting down to the lowest possible speed and keeping his eyes wide open for signs of impending ambush, Slater tooled the Flairboot into the mouth of the narrow estuary.

Coasting along now under conventional propulsive means, he followed the brackish water into the shadows cast by dense jungle foliage for about a quarter of a mile before the watercourse branched off into a dog-leg channel.

Slater followed the second branch, then another and still another, getting deeper and deeper into the dark labyrinth of mangrove islands.

Still he couldn't see hide nor hair of Ryecroft. The only discernible movements were the monkeys and brightly plumaged tropical birds flitting through the mesh of intertwining branches overhead.

Slater killed the engine and cautiously listened to the sounds around him. They told him that the jungle's calm had been recently disrupted. Bird calls and the movements of arboreal animals were certain indicators of human presence. Something had gone down this channel in the past few minutes.

Slater scoured the area carefully as he cautiously navigated up the silt-choked channel. He noticed the telltale breaks in low-hanging branches to either side, as well as the displacement of duckweed and other water plants that could have only been made by a boat passing through minutes before.

Now he was certain that he was finally on Ryecroft's track. The headman of the base was somewhere close by. In fact, he could be anywhere at all.

Maybe even right behind him.

MASON HAWKE LOBBED an antipersonnel grenade and covered the toss with pulsed bursts of Ultimax fire while Bishop hot-wired the truck. Under intense but inaccurate fire thrown by Carne's mercs, they sped off toward the airstrip where the Beech Duke was revving up for an emergency takeoff.

By now Kladen and his two fellow Berliners were on board the aircraft. They had to be taken down before they got the Beech airborne and were out of the range of SLAM's brand of justice. More important, they couldn't be allowed to warn Carne of the surprise operation mounted against him.

Busting the truck through the base perimeter fence, Hawke zoomed the Toyota flatbed pickup toward the light, fast plane. The Duke was already taxiing into position to roll down the runway. As the two commandos approached the aircraft, they were greeted by AK-47 fire from the open rear hatchway.

Heavy-caliber bullets smashed through the truck's windshield, and a round scored a hit on the Toyota's radiator, sending clouds of steam hissing up through the ruptured hood.

Hunched behind the cab in the truck bed, Eddie Bishop was already beating out a slug tattoo on the pintle-mounted .50-caliber Browning machine gun the truck was equipped with.

His first burst augered into the flank of the Beech's hull, leaving a zigzagging line of pockmarks along the side of the plane.

Fire from the Duke abruptly ceased for a spell as the door gunner pulled back into the safety of the cabin. Then the flash of the AK-47's muzzle spitting out another brace of bullets marked the start of a sustained burst of enfilading fire.

Hawke stomped hard on the gas pedal as the accelerating Beech picked up velocity and began to hover off the surface of the runway.

It was moments away from achieving lift and becoming fully airborne. The plane had to be stopped immediately or it would make it into the sky.

Hawke gained speed and passed the Duke while Bishop swung around the barrel of the Browning to fire a flanking burst at the side of the plane.

This time the burst was dead on target.

The AK-47 gunman in the hatchway shuddered violently as the heavy-caliber rounds thudded into his upper torso and head.

His death scream was cut short by the crazed ratcheting of his out-of-control Kalashnikov as the shooter's face disappeared in a bloody mist. With his brain shot away, control of the merc's body reverted to low-level nerve ganglia.

The bloodied corpse of the gunman hung by some magic onto the frame of the hatch, but in moments dropped away and thudded to the ground where it bounced and rolled as the Beech sped past it. The second gunman then jumped into position and cranked off more rounds from a second Kalashnikov autorifle.

By now Hawke had passed the nose of the aircraft. He caught a glimpse of Kladen's face framed in the cockpit window. The German did a double take as he spotted Hawke and hunched down to reach for something on the copilot's seat beside him.

Kladen whipped from concealment an Ingram SMG, opened the cockpit window and jammed the barrel of the MAC-10 through it. He cut loose with a burst at Hawke, which forced the SLAM commando to quickly fishtail the speedballing truck out of the line of fire.

Now the Beech shot past the stalled Toyota, outdistancing it in a cloud of dust. Its landing gear bounced off the uneven surface of the gravel runway, and its wings juddered in the airstream that was lifting it higher and higher.

In seconds it had risen five, six, then ten feet off the surface of the runway.

The German was airborne!

21

Slater idled the Flairboot cautiously up to a fork in the watercourse where the streams branched left and right. As yet he couldn't pick up the other craft's trail. Overhead the soft rustling of the forest canopy was disturbed every so often by the hooting of birds.

Suddenly automatic fire cut through the usual jungle sounds.

Whipping to starboard, Slater saw the muzzle-flashes from the other Flairboot, which was partially concealed by overhanging tree branches on the right bank of the channel.

Ryecroft was firing the AUG from the catbird seat. The sharp crackle and pop of ejecting rounds, followed by the *whap-whap* of steel-jacketed copper punching through shallow water into the silty bottom, as the 5.56 mm slugs were cranked out came closer and closer as Ryecroft walked his fire Slater's way.

He jumped from the Flairboot into the muddy water just as his boat went up in a balloon of scorching yellow flame. Soaked to the skin but still carrying the

M-16A2, he scrambled for cover behind some nearby rocks.

Slater now caught sight of Ryecroft jumping into the water and pushing his own Flairboot away from the protection of drooping mangrove branches where he'd hidden out. The man was shouldering his AUG, apparently thinking that he no longer needed bullets to kill his opponent. All he had to do was escape and leave Slater to rot in the middle of the steamy tropical hell.

Slater had no intention of being the odd man out. As Ryecroft splashed through the mud, about to climb into the Flairboot, he cut loose with a 40 mm grenade can that slammed into the side of the muddy embankment near Ryecroft's position.

Rocked by the blast, Ryecroft lost his footing and slipped into the brackish water. Slater didn't give him a chance to recover his bearings. With the M-16A2 studded on full-auto, he let the Aussie have it with a long burst of 5.56 mm steel.

Now cut off from the boat and unable to deploy his weapon because he was exposed in the open, Ryecroft had only a single option, and he took it. Breaking for cover, the merc stumbled through the water and clawed his way up the side of the mangrove island and into the brush, entirely forgetting about his boat. Right behind him, Slater waded across the shallow stream, throwing 5.56 mm fire at the fleeing man as he splashed through the channel.

Ryecroft disappeared into a mass of tangled vegetation, and Slater heard the ruckus he made as he went crashing off through the high spear grass and mangrove forest.

Slater gained the mangrove-choked embankment just behind the fleeing mercenary soldier. He had him cold.

"Ryecroft!" he called out as he sighted the M-16 on the Aussie's back. "Hold it right there, partner!"

Ryecroft's response was to spin on his heels and fire a hip-level burst from the AUG autoweapon that was both fast and accurate enough to have killed Slater had he not already sprinted from harm's way.

Forced to retreat by the surprise move, Slater had no choice but to tuck for cover and allow Ryecroft to gain more ground. Nevertheless, the man had as many places to go as Slater did. Without the Flairboot he, too, was as good as stranded on the tiny mangrove island.

Slater was up and running after Ryecroft a moment after the echo of the AUG rounds faded from earshot.

By now Ryecroft was badly winded, running out of steam. He had little choice but to dig in his heels and make a last stand. He raised the AUG and launched a burst of automatic fire at Slater, who dodged out of the blitzing line of tumblers and shot a 40 mm canister round at Ryecroft in swift response.

The round hit with a loud ka-rrrump. Ryecroft was caught in the shrapnel's killing radius and was instantly dismembered. Sheared away at the sockets and joints, parts of his limbs were blown across the sodden jungle floor. Slater scrambled over to his maimed foe and looked down at the broken thing that had once been a man.

There was just enough left of Ryecroft for the merc to communicate to Slater the incredible pain he was suffering.

Slater understood the pleading look in the dying man's glazing eyes. It was a look he had seen many times before in different places. A look that meant only one thing.

Lowering the barrel, Slater triggered a mercy burst of steel that blew away the mortally wounded man's head and put him out of his misery forever.

HAWKE STOMPED the pickup's gas pedal to the floorboards and pulled the Toyota abreast of the Beech's cockpit, seemingly more by force of conscious will than by virtue of the mathematical laws of physical dynamics.

Behind him in the bed of the highballing truck, Eddie Bishop swung the barrel of the .50-caliber machine gun into snuff position and cranked out a burst at the

second gunman who'd popped into the rear doorway
of the cabin.

The gunman's AK-47 bratted 7.62 mm bursts at
Bishop. The javelin of whizzing steel hurled by the Kalashnikov came damn close to scoring, but in this game
only the bull's-eyes counted.

Bishop rough-spotted through the Browning's sights
and triggered another long burst that zigzagged across
the plane's fuselage, passing the hatchway, and jack-
hammered his fire toward the Beech's tail assembly.

As the jagged line of .50-caliber slugs moved along
the fuselage, it razored across the belt line of the gunman framed in the open bulkhead. The German merc
went spastic and was catapulted back into the shadows of the passenger compartment by the force of the
blast like a puppet yanked by unseen strings.

The heavy-caliber bullets sprayed by the big .50
chewed away at the rear ailerons of the rising plane.
Robbed of its maneuverability, the Duke became unstable. High-octane aviation fuel was now spilling from
the ruptured tanks in a thick stream.

Kladen fought the controls to govern the airborne
plane's angle of climb. But the Duke wobbled errati-
cally as it gained altitude, and there wasn't a hell of a
lot the German could do at this point.

Bishop swung the barrel of the Browning upward
and triggered a put-away burst. He saw the glowing

tracers impact against the underbelly of the wobbling, pitching aircraft and punch right through the floor of the cockpit.

The burst came smashing up through the pilot's seat and continued traveling through the German's body cavity, fragmenting on pelvic bone and ripping his entrails to shreds. Mortally wounded, the chemist lost consciousness and collapsed against the controls, the weight of his dying body pushing them forward.

Now the plane nosed down as it simultaneously swerved to one side. Bishop's line of .50-caliber bullets moved on toward the tail assembly until a glowing tracer struck the ruptured fuel tank. The entire rear section of the plane exploded in midair, blowing apart in a spinning fireball of wreckage doused in burning aviation fuel.

Moments later the cockpit and wings of the aircraft crashed headlong into the jungle trees at the edge of the runway with a deafening report. This wreckage, too, was already burning fiercely.

The shattered hulk of the Duke's airframe hung tangled in the treetops for a couple of seconds and then suddenly went up with an earsplitting bang as the Duke broke up into dozens of pinwheeling fireballs and a yellow mushroom of flame rose hundreds of feet into the cloudless blue sky.

Bishop let the overheated barrel sag down, and Hawke swung the truck back toward the base. Leaning on the big gun, Bishop wiped his sweaty forehead with his sleeve as the truck raced through a pall of acrid black smoke thrown up by the scattered pieces of burning wreckage littering the runway.

22

Slater had a difficult time navigating back out of the maze of muddy channels and small islands. Hours had passed since he'd taken off after the fleeing chief of the coke facility. By now Slater was wondering what had become of Hawke and Bishop.

Guiding the Flairboot back down the main tributary of the river, Slater navigated against the current toward the base.

Once he was out of the boondocks and on the main channel again, finding the base posed no problem. The immense plume of black smoke towering up into the sky marked the position of the base for miles in every direction as clearly as a lighthouse beacon.

Slater found the entire installation in shambles when he hopped off his transport and onto the planks of the pontoon dock. It was already midmorning, and Hawke and Bishop had herded the survivors of the assault into groups of prisoners. These were mostly Carne's native *coqueros* who, with their weapons taken away, wore the downtrodden expressions of unprincipled men completely broken in spirit.

Slater found Hawke and Bishop standing guard over the group of prisoners whom they had stockaded in a big hole about twenty feet deep and thirty feet in diameter, which had been ripped out of the jungle floor by the detonation of the solvent drums.

Slater smiled as he caught sight of his two partners, glad to see they were both alive and well.

"You two did a pretty fair night's work," he told them. "Hit any snags?"

"Not much," Bishop replied. "Only our friend Kladen gave us some trouble. Seems he wanted to leave the party early."

"Did you stop him?"

"Stopped him cold," Hawke responded. "But you can forget about using the Duke to fly out of this hellhole," he went on. "We had to take the plane down to get the German."

"Damn," lamented Slater, who'd been counting on the Beech in order to facilitate SLAM's own extraction. "Damn, damn, damn."

SLATER, HAWKE AND BISHOP drove one of the captured trucks formerly belonging to Carne's *coqueros* into the nearest town, where they learned that a plane could be chartered.

The plane was of World War II vintage, a superannuated Ford Trimotor transport aircraft that had seen better days when GIs stormed the Anzio beachhead.

The pilot seemed as old as the plane and looked as though he'd seen a couple of better days, too. The commandos soon found out that they'd have to share the ride with a couple of crates of chickens and two enormous hogs.

But the plane was the only available method of fast transportation back to Carne's baronial estate in the northern mountain regions, and SLAM was forced to hire out the old pilot's services. Money changed hands, and Slater and company went on board, and in a short while the plane taxied bumpily down the runway and barely made it into the air.

The rest of the forty-minute flight was rocky but otherwise survivable. The transport set down again at an airstrip a few miles outside of Carne's home base. By some miracle, the crude airstrip was equipped with a working pay telephone that actually made and received calls.

Slater dialed the number and was soon on the horn to Carne himself.

As Slater had expected, Carne sounded fit to chew the rug. The Colombian narcobaron had already received reports of the fiasco at his forest drug refinery.

He had been trying to find out what had gone down for hours, with little success.

"What the hell is happening, Slater?" he demanded loudly. "How bad is the damage?"

"The damn DEA and the Colombian paramilitary narcs," Slater told him. "They pulled a surprise raid on the installation."

"Impossible!" Carne shouted into the handset. "I pay millions of dollars in protection money. Do you think just the Colombians take payoffs? Your DEA alone gets millions!"

"Easy, Carne," Slater growled. "We're on an open line. For all I know, it was the little green men from Mars who came down to kick some ass. Besides, it doesn't mean shit to me. I just work here. You call the shots, not me."

"Okay, okay," Carne continued, calming down a little. "It's not your fault." Slater thought he heard ice cubes clinking and Carne swallowing in the background. "Your men, did they get out okay?" the druglord next wanted to know.

"Hawke and Bishop were both KIA as far as I can tell," Slater said, looking across the airstrip at his two partners kibitzing with the old pilot. "As far as I was concerned, it was every man for himself."

"I'll send a car for you," Carne said, sounding like his old businesslike self again. "You sit tight until my driver gets to the airport, *comprende?*"

"I read you, amigo," Slater said, and racked the receiver. Then he walked across the dusty airfield to join Hawke and Bishop by the plane and outline the rest of the plan.

SLATER WATCHED the rickety old transport taxi down the runway and take off with Hawke and Bishop in the passenger compartment. The two SLAM commandos would provide backup in the coming final phase of the mission to take Carne out of the running.

The plane's new destination was to be the Colombian capital of Bogotá, where Hawke and Bishop could hook up with Intelligence support people and arrange for matériel, transport and the fresh Intel needed for the next round of SLAM-style housecleaning.

Pretty soon Slater saw the air-conditioned Mercedes limousine pull up. He cracked the rear door and climbed in the back seat. The sullen driver didn't say anything, and Slater settled back to enjoy the scenery through tinted windows.

There wasn't a lot to see except for monotonous miles of unbroken jungle and twisting brown dirt road. Slater had had a bellyful of both by now.

Forty-five minutes of driving over the bumpiest and most rutted roads this side of Tranquility Base One,

Slater pulled into the high gates of Carne's mansion, rolled past the emerald pastures where the narcolord's prize Spanish ponies were grazing and climbed out of the back seat of the Mercedes town car to walk toward the mansion's high front doors.

Beyond the ornately carved hardwood portals the inviting coolness of a traditional Spanish-style hacienda greeted him. One of Carne's liveried manservants was already waiting there, handing him a cool drink and suggesting that he go out back to the poolside area where Carne was waiting.

Slater found the druglord in his bathing trunks, swimming a couple of laps in the Olympic-size swimming pool.

All things considered, he had to hand it to the guy. Carne's entire drug operation—a project he'd sunk countless millions of bucks into and had taken him years of hard work to put together—had just gone up in smoke, and yet there he was, swimming laps as cool as if antifreeze flowed through his veins instead of blood.

Slater took a seat at a white enameled patio table beneath the shade of a beach umbrella and sipped white tequila and lime juice as Carne hauled himself out of the pool and toweled himself dry. He snatched a fresh margarita from a servant's tray and seated himself opposite Slater.

"What happened?" Carne asked as he sipped at the drink, holding the glass in one hand and toweling his hair with the other. "Tell me. All of it. Take your time."

"Not much to tell," Slater replied calmly. "The excrement hit the old whirling blades around 4:00 a.m. Night drop by trained paratroops. They were out for blood. Shot first, asked questions later. You must have gotten some heavy people pretty damn pissed, Carne."

Carne sipped his drink and regarded Slater through gimlet eyes, which noted his unshaven, combat-stained face and torn clothes, the slouch of a man who hadn't slept in several days, the whites of his gray eyes shot through with angry veins of red.

"You look like you've been through hell," he said. "We'll talk more later."

"Great," Slater said as he stood up to go, "I can use a shower."

"No," Carne told him, shaking his head. "No shower for you. Not till I've cleared up a few questions with the proper authorities."

Slater saw Carne flick his finger at an unseen presence behind him. Next thing, he felt the muzzle of a gun jammed in the small of his back.

"My great-great-grandfather built this place with his bare hands," Carne went on, coolly sipping his margarita as he looked up at Slater with eyes gone hard.

"He had to deal not only with hostile *Indios* but with treacherous gringos like yourself. Neither could be trusted. In those days, as now, a landowner made his own laws. My illustrious grandfather built quite an elaborate dungeon below."

Rogelio la Carne waved to the gunman, who force-marched Slater away. "I regret that there are no showers available there," he concluded.

23

A secure telex to Pentagon liaison officer Jack Callixto was all it took for a specially outfitted Blackhawk helicopter to be placed at the disposal of Hawke and Bishop.

Bishop pulled sky-jockey duty while Hawke strapped himself into the side gunner's rig behind the chopper's pintle-mounted 7.62 mm Minigun. Both had been checked out to fly the warbird, but riding shotgun was a matter of Hawke's personal preference.

Navigating the Blackhawk by means of the AN/PVS-7A night-vision imaging and target-acquisition system, Bishop effortlessly glided the multirole combat chopper on a low-trajectory flight path across the top of the jungle tree line.

The two shadow warriors had set out from the covert border LZ approximately an hour earlier, extra fuel on board. Estimated flight time to their destination—the northern ranges of Colombia and Carne's hacienda—was another thirty-five minutes.

That gave both of them an opportunity to get their weapons and gear in order. While Hawke's Minigun could crank out the 7.62 mm slugs with a speed unmatched by any other weapon short of a Vulcan cannon, Bishop had at his disposal pylon-mounted Hellfire missiles.

Internal diagnostic routines indicated to Bishop that all the chopper's weapon systems were reading in the green, while Hawke made sure that the Minigun's belt-feed mechanism and other working parts checked out clean and mean with no margin for error in between.

The name of the game this morning was bust out and bust up. Bust Slater out of Carne's hardbase and bust up the narcobaron's operation for good. Put the major-league coke trafficker out of business.

Put him beyond salvage.

DEAL SLATER KNEW Hawke and Bishop were coming for him, but he didn't know precisely when and he didn't know exactly how. All he could do was sit tight in his dungeon cell and wait it out until his backup got into position.

But Carne had other ideas about what Slater's ultimate fate would be, to say nothing of the timetable he alloted to it. Slater was rudely awakened just before dawn by a pair of grim Colombian buttonmen who threw open his cell door and told Slater to come with them.

Slater had no doubts that his moment of reckoning was quickly approaching. He could tell these guys were fixing to drill a bullet into the back of his head and dump him in a ditch somewhere.

Years ago he'd seen facial expressions identical to the ones they wore. Only then it had been on the faces of Salvadorans in the service of the ruling military junta's roving death squads. Slater didn't have to do any hard thinking to know that Carne had just handed down an order to have him chilled.

Slater's two new playmates shoved him forward down a musty-smelling stone corridor, around a dogleg bend, then down a flight of stone steps into a deeper level of the subbasement of Carne's ancestral home.

Here was a warren of catacombs with an arched vault overhead, very cool and very dark, lit here and there by the occasional naked bulb. It was the type of place good for two things: aging fine wine or burying bodies.

Slater didn't happen to see any wine racks anywhere. Just an old shovel leaned up against the sweating stone wall of the arch-ceilinged chamber where his two grim-faced warders had brought him.

"Dig," one of the two gunmen ordered him in English, pantomiming with his hands just in case the *norteamericano* didn't get the message. Slater picked up the shovel and began to turn the earth.

First he jammed the spade into the hard-packed floor, then he pulled up a heap of dirt, then he piled the dirt to one side and repeated the process.

Shove it in, pull it out, pile it up.

Once, twice, three times.

He wanted to keep up the same steady, monotonous pace until the thug with the Colt .45 ACP pistol pointed at his head had gotten just a little bit too used to the rhythm of the condemned man's movements than was healthy for him.

Shove it in, pull it out, pile it up.

Four, five, six times.

The next shovel load went right into the hardman's face.

The suddenly blinded man yelled and brought up his .45 semiauto for a put-away shot. Slater followed through, quickly swinging the flat of the shovel at the torpedo and feeling it connect with the upraised gun in his hand.

A second whack of the shovel sent rusty iron crunching into brittle cheekbones and nasal cartilage to completely cave in the front of the clobbered thug's face.

Blood spilling out of his head and pouring down his shirt, the gunman stood there reeling dazedly and yelling in rapid-fire Spanish. Slater booted him hard in the keister and sent him sprawling into the partly dug grave, where he lay groaning and squirming.

The second would-be executioner had come running and was already aiming his pistol at Slater, who dodged and weaved and zigzagged, making it hard for the shooter to draw an accurate bead on him while Slater at the same time charged forward.

Once Slater was close enough, he used a hard arm block to deflect the gun hand of the shooter and drove the steel tip of his jump boot between the man's legs with enough force to crush his testicles.

Wild-eyed with pain, the assassin grunted and sagged to the floor. Slater snatched up his firearm and discovered that the Colt .45 ACP contained a full clip of hollowpoints but no live steel in the pipe. Slater pulled back the semiauto weapon's slide and corrected that sorry deficiency.

He was just in time. The moment he rounded the corridor, he came smack up against two more of Carne's strong-arm men. Catching sight of Slater, they pulled side iron from holsters at their hips.

But the Colt was already gripped in Slater's hands, cranking out accurate fire. The fusillade of slugs struck the targets with devastating results. The first of the two enforcers lost control of his body and went crashing into the stone wall behind him, then he slid down into a kneeling position.

The second torpedo caught a faceful of spinning steel that tore away half his cheek and laid bare the bright pink musculature and gleaming white bone underneath amid a shower of dark red blood.

The gunman let out a cry as he crashed face-first onto the flagstone floor of the tunnel and lay there, bleeding profusely. Slater was about to move on when the downed triggerman suddenly rolled over with a gun in his hand.

Slater nailed him through the forehead with a well-placed round and hastened along the tunnel. He was cutting nobody slack today.

THE BLACKHAWK popped up over the tree line a moment before Carne's perimeter guards spotted it. One minute nothing was there but a bunch of trees. The next, something big and mean looking was staring them right in the face.

That was the way it was when flying nap-of-the-earth. Now you don't see it, now you do.

This time it was too late for the security squad.

The narcobaron's hired muscle raised their heat as the gunship "unmasked" above the tree line but were cut down by a whizzing storm that cycled from the muzzle of the chattering Minigun in the chopper's open bay door.

As the dying sentinels hit the ground bleeding and thrashing, the Blackhawk moved on, its underbelly mere feet off the deck. Hovering the gunship now, Bishop triggered a Hellfire round that slammed into the side of the hacienda, blowing away most of its red-clay-tiled roof.

Thick, acrid smoke billowed up from the ruptured roof in a massive cloud. Bishop swung the combat chopper full around as more gunmen spilled out of the house like angry soldier ants rushing to defend their threatened hive. Dots and dashes of blue muzzle flame broke the darkness of the night as Carne's protectors fired their automatic weapons up at the chopper.

Unfortunately for them, they could barely see the helicopter against the sky whereas the men overhead were equipped with night-vision equipment. Bishop fired another Hellfire salvo into the dense center of the hit squad and blew most of the Colombian war party away in a flash of phosphorescent white.

When the opposition had dwindled, Bishop set the Blackhawk down for a landing. Unfastening his harness, he grabbed up the M-60E3 lying across the copilot's seat beside him and climbed out of the pilot's chair. Hawke was already out ahead of him, an Ultimax clutched in his fists as he bolted toward the huge hole blown in the side of the baronial manor, a battle cry on his lips.

24

The thunder of explosions was like music to Slater's ears. The big bangs of detonating Hellfire warheads meant that his SLAM backup had arrived on scene with near to perfect timing.

As Slater zigzagged through the catacombs searching for a way topside, though, he headed straight into an ambush.

The gunman was hustling down a flight of stone stairs just around one of the many bends in the tortuously twisting tunnel system. Slater spotted the shooter just as he was about to level the Kalashnikov he gripped with white-knuckled tension.

The big American moved fast, throwing his body to the stone deck and performing a swift half roll that brought him under the gunner's sights. Extending his arms from a horizontal stretch and clutching the pistol in both hands, Slater triggered a .45-caliber bullet right into the shooter's midsection.

The gut-shot torpedo dropped his autorifle as he tumbled down the stairs and onto the flagstone floor.

Slater helped himself to the AK-47 the gunman had been about to fire at him.

Now packing the Kalashnikov, Slater kicked in the door to a communications room and hosed down the interior. The radioman and his partner had just reached the paramilitary police barracks assigned to the province and were about to send out a call for assistance.

Spotting the intruder, they lunged for their weapons, but they were too slow and were sent swiftly to meet their makers by the jackhammering 7.62 mm slammers fired by the bucking gun in Slater's fists.

Slater let the radio equipment have it with a second volley of Kalashnikov steel, firing until the weapon's 30-round banana clip had completely run dry.

He found two spare magazines for the dead mercs' rifles, as well as three other spare 30-round banana clips in their pockets.

Slater cranked a fresh mag into the receiver of the Kalashnikov and hustled out of the commo room and back into the tunnel. His objective was now twofold: to link up with Hawke and Bishop and to get his sights aimed at Carne.

Up till now it had just been business.

But not anymore.

Carne had tried to whack Slater out.

Carne had made it personal.

THE ULTIMAX CLUTCHED in Mason Hawke's fists cranked off a toxic 5.56 mm blizzard. The autoburst of steel-jacketed tumblers brought down the guards stationed inside the ruined hacienda. Eddie Bishop was already inside the big manor house, his M-60E3 blazing out a cyclone of chattering autofire.

Slater had made tracks to the poolside area when he spun around to catch sight of Hawke stepping into view with the muzzle of the Ultimax pointed his way.

"About time you guys showed up," he told Hawke. "You saw Carne?"

"Nope," Hawke responded. "Haven't seen hide nor hair of him."

"That's what I was afraid you'd say," Slater returned. He'd been putting the boot to doors for the past fifteen minutes without any luck.

He'd been upstairs in Carne's bedroom complex and downstairs in his private screening room, wet bar and gymnasium. The poolside was the last place he figured to look because it was the most exposed and therefore offered the smallest chance that Carne would be found there.

This turn of events meant that Carne had pulled a vanishing act on them.

Just then Bishop came running up to join Slater and Hawke.

"Big APC just roared out of the main gate," he said, slightly out of breath. "I fired a couple of rounds at it but I couldn't touch it. A Saxon or a Unimog," he added. "Couldn't be sure, though. Too hard to see through all the smoke."

A little light bulb went on in Slater's brain. He had no doubt that inside that personnel carrier was his quarry.

"Did you two fly the chopper in as planned?" Slater asked. When Hawke replied in the affirmative, Slater told them to mop up the remainder of Carne's scattered forces. He was going to go after the escaping vehicle in the Blackhawk.

THE FAST, maneuverable combat helicopter lifted off from the inner compound of the manor house. Though Slater's teammates had fired off Hellfire missiles, there were still enough left in the chopper's side-mounted external stores support—ESS—clusters to take out the APC.

Slater banked the Hawk on a sixty-degree flight vector and skimmed the treetops above the narrow, twisting mountain road. The steady *whump-whump-whump* of the rotors overhead and the steady whine of the turbines told him better than any instrument panel chiclets that the gunship's on-board systems were functioning normally.

It wasn't long before he picked up the trail of the APC, which was moving as slow as molasses in relation to the chopper's cruising speed.

Bishop's first guess turned out to be correct. The personnel carrier *was* a Saxon. British-made, tough as they came.

Originally developed for high-hazard duty in Northern Ireland as a replacement for the infamous "Pig," the APC had been designed to withstand anything that might likely be thrown at it. This Saxon was a new and better breed, too, equipped with smoke grenade launchers and a 7.62 mm turret-mounted machine gun.

Pulling up on the collective and easing forward the cyclic pitch stick while using foot pedals to control the Hawk's tail rotor, Slater gained altitude and launched a Hellfire from a stationary hover. The rocket hissed from the ESS cluster, hardly yawing the chopper, and hit the ground moments later. The round scored a near-miss, though, and as far as killing the Saxon went, a near-miss was as good as a mile.

In answer to his rocket salvo, automatic fire blazed from gun ports at the left and right flanks of the heavily armored vehicle while the 7.62 mm machine gun up top cranked out a continuous salvo of steel.

A heavy-caliber round in the right spot could very well blow the Blackhawk clean out of the sky. Slater jinked to one side and gained altitude as he prepared to launch a second missile.

INSIDE THE SAXON, Carne peered anxiously out through one of the frontal observation ports equipped with bulletproof glass as tough as the armored steel of the vehicular hull. Beside him were three of his security men manning the APC's gun ports. He could hear the powerful high-pitched roar of the Blackhawk's four rotor blades as they revolved overhead.

"Blow the bastard out of the sky," Carne shouted as he produced an inhaler from his pocket and snorted some crystalline coke.

The gunman nearest Carne turned from the gun port and stared down the drug baron with cold, flat eyes filled with hate and contempt.

"Shut up," he spit out.

Carne recoiled in shock and amazement. "How dare you address me in such a manner?" he shouted in anger. "Do you realize who you are speaking to?"

The hardman flicked out his hand and knocked the inhaler from Carne's grasp. The other two snickered and did nothing to intervene. Who gave a damn? They were all dead men anyway.

In a single, almost effortless motion, the gunman shoved Carne against the wall and jammed the muzzle of his AKM into Carne's face. The red-hot gun barrel blistered the skin and started the druglord's nose smoking, giving off a revolting stench.

"I am speaking to a useless cur," he rasped. "A miserable dog who will keep his mouth shut from now on."

Carne shrank back in terror as the hardman withdrew the gun and turned his back on him, as did the others with malicious smiles on their perspiration-filmed faces. Carne shivered and shook all over. He sat on the vehicle's deck and held his head in his hands, moaning in pain and inhaling the foul odor of his own hideously scorched flesh.

NOW ABOVE the personnel carrier, the Blackhawk's Hellfire targeting system acquired a solid lock on the Saxon. But before Slater could fire his round, the APC began popping smoke and was soon enveloped in a dense white cloud, then it abruptly went around a bend and was hidden from view beneath the dense canopy of jungle trees.

The Hellfire lock was lost, at least temporarily. Slater had no choice but to overfly the road and wait until he was next positioned for a cleaner shot at the Saxon. Minutes later the APC emerged from the cover of the trees back onto a ruler-straight stretch of road.

Finally Slater was cleared for a strike.

Slater hovered the chopper and launched a Hellfire missile. The rocket whooshed down to slam into the rear of the Saxon. This time its warhead detonated right on target and blasted a mammoth gash in the Saxon's heavily armored hull.

THE LAST EARTHLY THING that Carne saw was the face of the hardman who had shoved the gun up his nose disintegrating into a shining starburst of blood.

Carne began to scream, but before the scream had time to gather, a whirling piece of white-hot, semimolten shrapnel tore away most of his throat, ripping out his vocal cords and leaving only a blood-jetting cavity behind.

A pulsebeat later the second Hellfire round blew the damaged APC to smithereens. The shattered wreckage shot upward in a fountain of jagged, flaming metal, then tumbled downward in hundreds of smoldering pieces.

25

The police commander wore a tailored military uniform. The visor of his cap sat low on his head, hooding eyes that missed nothing. Yet his bearing was relaxed, that of a man not accustomed to allowing difficulties to cramp his style.

"Señor Slater," he said. "You gringos are giving me one hell of a problem."

Slater was seated in the commander's office in front of a large desk of gleaming walnut. He, but not his SLAM colleagues, had been scooped up by the paracops who had arrived just after Slater had dealt with the Saxon.

When he had touched down at the smoldering ruins of the baronial estate, the place was swarming with local paramilitary cops.

Slater hadn't seen any trace of Hawke and Bishop and figured that either the police had already taken them into custody or they'd taken off, which was the more likely of the two possibilities.

No matter how fast or maneuverable the Blackhawk chopper was, it was still no match for a military jet—even the outdated hardware flown by the Colombian air force. Slater had figured his best bet was to touch down and bullshit the cops.

But no way would he allow them to get their hands on a sophisticated piece of machinery like the Blackhawk. Slater had activated the helo's auto-destruct feature, rose into the air again and swung the chopper in the other direction, as though he were trying to escape, and disappeared over the tree line.

A quarter mile from the site of the bombed-out mansion he'd jumped into a clearing from a low hover and from the cover of a boulder watched the Blackhawk sail into the trees, where it exploded moments later.

As he'd climbed to his feet and begun walking back in the direction of the hacienda, a paramilitary police Range Rover had come roaring up the road.

"Why did you try to escape?" the cop had asked the gringo in Spanish.

Slater's reply, in idiomatic American English, had been to allude to a certain bodily function that he had preferred performing against a tree rather than out the window of the chopper.

"I don't understand," the cop had replied in Spanish.

With an engaging smile, Slater had then made a comment unflattering to the purity of the questioner's ancestral bloodline.

"I don't understand," the perplexed cop had responded again, and hauled Slater off into the Range Rover for questioning by somebody who spoke some *Yanqui* talk. From there on in, Slater had been shuffled around from one minor official to another. All along, he'd told his questioners only two things.

The first was that he didn't know anything about the fate of Señor Rogelio la Carne. The second was that they should take him immediately to the chief of police. Eventually, after cooling his heels in a hot jail cell that stank of sweat and urine, Slater found himself sitting in the office of the city of Cali's police commander.

He had been sticking to the story that he was Señor Carne's personal bodyguard, who had been trying to save his employer's life.

How he'd gotten hold of a sophisticated piece of gringo combat gear was another matter, although the chief of paramilitary police didn't put anything past a man like Señor Carne and the power of his enormous wealth.

Slater reached forward and took a cigarette from the pearl-inlaid humidor atop the desk. They were American smokes.

"You mind?"

"Help yourself," the police chief offered. He reached inside his pocket and gave Slater a light from a gold cigarette lighter. The huge emerald on the gold ring he wore didn't escape Slater's attention. Here was a man who appreciated the finer things in life, these accoutrements declared.

"Like I was telling you," Slater went on, taking a drag on the cigarette, "somebody hit Carne. I don't have to tell you that my former employer had his share of enemies, as well as friends. It could have been the DEA, it could have been another group trying to muscle in on him, it could have been practically anybody."

"But you don't have any idea who specifically?" the commander said, eyeing Slater skeptically as he leaned back in his high-backed leather chair.

"No idea at all," Slater replied with a smile.

The man spread his hands in exasperation as he leaned forward again.

"As I have told you, Señor Slater," he said, "you are an embarrassment, a problem. I have spoken with your embassy. They don't want to hear about you. I have spoken with my superiors. They have dumped the entire matter into my lap. I wish to heaven I had never seen you."

"Then make one more phone call," Slater advised. "To a guy named Francisco Terra Nova in Mexico. Terra Nova can fix things."

The police chief's eyes narrowed. He had heard of Terra Nova.

"You know this man Terra Nova?" he asked Slater. "Personally know him?"

"Make the call," Slater told him. "Or let me make it."

The commander handed Slater the phone on his desk. Minutes later Slater had punched in the direct call to Terra Nova's cellular link.

The Mexican druglord answered quickly. Slater heard the sounds of traffic in the background. Terra Nova was cruising down some highway in Mexico in an expensive set of wheels, he figured. Smart as Terra Nova was, he didn't even know what was going down.

"Got some bad news for you, boss," Slater said. "Carne's operation was hit. La Carne's been wasted."

There was silence on the other end of the line. Then Terra Nova spoke in an even voice.

"I already know something about this turn of events," he replied emotionlessly. "I would certainly like to talk to you about it at greater length. How can we meet?"

Just like old Francisco, Slater thought to himself. Always concerned about the line being bugged. Always cool, always slick. But he was riding for a hard fall just the same.

"Hold on a minute," Slater said into the handset. "Got a guy here who wants to talk to you."

Slater handed the police chief the phone, and the man conversed in Spanish with Terra Nova. A couple of minutes later he put down the handset and looked up at Slater, who could tell right away that the man was very much relieved.

"I never saw you," the cop said, tearing up the report on his desk and hitting the intercom button. A few moments later his uniformed gofer appeared at the door, his fingers rising to his red beret in a military-style salute. "Take this gringo pain-in-the-ass to the airport," he instructed. "See that he gets on the next flight to Mexico."

26

Terra Nova's Mercedes limousine was waiting for Slater at the Guadalajara airport on his return flight from Bogotá. From there he rode in air-conditioned comfort to the Octagon, where the boss was anxiously awaiting his arrival, eager to have a sit-down.

Slater found the druglord dressed in his usual fashionable attire, impeccably groomed and redolent of expensive men's cologne. Terra Nova seemed in high spirits, acting as if he were glad to see his returning warrior and greeting him like a long-lost friend.

He was acting in a way that put Slater on guard because he had learned that with individuals like Terra Nova, the way they acted was usually the opposite of the way they felt.

Throwing his arm around Slater's neck, Terra Nova ushered him into his office. Slater saw jewelry glitter on his fingers and at his throat and caught another fragrant whiff of the expensive men's cologne.

"I'm glad you got out okay despite some serious problems," Terra Nova said to his security chief. "Now

I want to hear everything. A full briefing. This is important. After all, amigo, whoever hit Carne may come after me next. I need to know what you think."

"Not much, I'm afraid," Slater said with a shrug. "Just that whoever it was brought a hell of a lot of firepower with them. They just blew Carne's operation to shit."

"I have been busy making inquiries," Terra Nova replied, looking at Slater across the tips of steepled fingers on which gold rings gleamed. "None of my contacts can confirm any such raid." His voice now had a distinctly steely edge to it, which Slater read as the equivalent of a stiletto blade snapping open.

"The DEA doesn't broadcast its plans," Slater told him evenly.

"Still, I have invested vast sums in maintaining a network of reliable informants," Terra Nova returned, his smiling eyes losing their mirth and going flat and distant. "It seems unlikely I would not know anything."

"Okay, so your high-priced pigeons didn't sing," Slater protested. "What can I tell you? You asked me about what went down. I told you. Can't do anything else."

"Yes, you can, I think," Terra Nova said with a smile, his eyes full of menace.

Suddenly his hands came up from below the desk. In his right he clutched a pearl-handled, chrome-finished .45-caliber automatic pistol. He pointed the business end of the piece at Slater while his other hand hit the intercom stud on his desk phone.

"Yes, *jefe?*" Slater heard the voice of Terra Nova's enforcer from the speaker grille.

"Bring Delgado," Terra Nova said smoothly. "Put Mr. Slater on ice until further notice."

SLATER HUNG from the ceiling of a pet-food cannery owned by Terra Nova in Ciudad Juarez, a stone's throw from the Texas border. Heavy chains were wound tightly around his wrists and secured to the hook at the end of a cable stretching down from a motorized winch bolted to the ceiling. Directly beneath him was the yawning feed hopper of a heavy-duty wood chipper.

Terra Nova stood below Slater, a little ways across the room. He had a broad grin on his aquiline face. Very soon Slater's minced remains would join animal remnants in giant vats and ultimately be canned as food for American house pets.

"Delgado, turn on the machine," he ordered his underling.

A deafening roar suddenly filled the cavernous interior of the deserted cannery as soon as the mechanism was activated. Terra Nova looked up at Slater with a broad smile.

"This wood chipper is top-of-the-line," he told Slater with bizarre pride. "You can't buy a better one. It can reduce a big log to sawdust in mere seconds. Let me give you a little demonstration."

Nearby was a bin full of scrap lumber from recent renovation on the cannery. Terra Nova searched through the pile until he had selected a two-by-four he deemed suitable to his ends.

He pitched the hunk of lumber into the wide-mouthed hopper at the top of the wood chipper. The grinding machine groaned and grunted, and a cloud of sawdust sprayed out through a chute below as the log disappeared into its voracious maw. Soon the roar of the machinery died away, and the two-by-four had been completely ground down to a heap of pulverized wood.

"I think you now can appreciate what this machine can do to human flesh, human bone...human muscle," Terra Nova declared after his demonstration. "For that reason I will make sure that you are lowered into it a little at a time."

"You're all heart, guy," Slater replied.

"And you'll soon be all mush," Terra Nova returned.

As he was speaking, Slater noticed that one of the hired muscle, a fat man named Rubio, or "Blondie," was setting up a video Camcorder on a tripod. Moments later Slater was forced to squint as the recording unit's bright halogen lights were switched on.

"But now I'll take my leave," the druglord declared. "What will happen to you will be messy. Frankly I'll enjoy it better on TV. That way I can fast-forward to the good parts."

Terra Nova exchanged a few sentences in Spanish with his enforcers and exited the cannery, leaving his men to finish Slater off.

Delgado, gaunt framed and dressed with his usual flash in a loose-fitting suit, already had the winch remote in his hand. He grinned up at Slater as he thumbed the button activating the winch's powerful motor.

Slater began dropping down until the soles of his boots were level with the rim of the chipper's feed hopper. The roaring began to build to an earsplitting crescendo as Terra Nova's enforcer eagerly prepared to lower him the rest of the way inside the furiously grinding machine.

27

Now Slater could feel the updraft generated by the rows of carbon-steel split hammers that revolved at high torque inches below the soles of his boots.

"Don't worry, gringo," the Mexican named Delgado said, shouting to be heard above the whine of the chopping machine, "it won't hurt so bad. If you have pain, you just sing out."

The Mexican thumbed the button on the remote-control unit clutched in his hand, and the ceiling-mounted winch paid out a foot of galvanized wire cable. He would enjoy watching Slater die. The gringo had killed his friend Montana on Manzanillo Beach—of this he was certain. It would be a pleasure to return the favor. Slowly.

Slater's guts churned as he dropped lower, then suddenly jerked to a swinging halt as Delgado took his thumb off the button, leaving him dangling with his feet below the upper edges of the feed hopper.

"How you feel, gringo?" the Mexican asked wolfishly. "You pissing your pants, maybe? You want to beg for your life, maybe? You—"

Suddenly the whine of the machine was punctuated by a series of popping noises, and the strong-arm man clutching the winch remote spun around with a sudden, unnatural movement. There was a gaping red hole ripped from the center of his chest, through which organ matter and blood was rapidly spewing, the result of multiple strikes by sound-suppressed automatic fire.

As the first man was taken down, the rotund Mexican who had been working the Camcorder reached for the Ingram M-11 hanging from his shoulder on a swivel mount.

Before he could bring the subgun into play, another round of suppressed slugs launched on full-auto tore a jagged puncture line across his paunchy midsection.

The Mexican torpedo gushed a crimson torrent and staggered on buckling legs. Knocking over the tripodmounted Camcorder, he collapsed into a bloody heap. From behind him, Venice, her blond mane flying behind her, sprinted toward the winch remote. She snatched it up from the the concrete floor and quickly threw it in reverse. In one hand she clutched an H&K MP-5 with the stubby cylinder of a suppressor projecting from its muzzle.

Slater began rising away from the whirling split hammers of the wood chipper. When he was well clear of the feed hopper, Venice crossed to him and switched off the machine.

In a short while Slater had both feet planted on the floor. Once the chains wrapped around his wrists had been taken from the winch hook, it was a simple matter to slip them off his hands.

Slater rubbed his wrists to start getting circulation back into his arms, then picked up the MAC-11 dropped by one of Terra Nova's enforcers.

He checked the weapon's clip, glad to find that the 32-round high-capacity magazine was loaded up with hollownose 9 mm slugs and that there was a live dumdum round already sitting in the chamber.

"Follow me," Venice told him. "There's a secret way out of here. A tunnel that leads across the border. Terra Nova had it built on the sly and told nobody about it."

"Except you, of course," Slater corrected.

"That's right," she affirmed with a nod. She peered around the corner of the L-shaped corridor opening from the doorway they had rushed through and motioned for Slater to proceed.

Slater followed the swiftly moving woman, keeping the MAC positioned at his hip to unleash rapid fire. Within minutes the pair had reached a dead end in the corridor. Confronting them now was a locked steel door.

Venice reached behind her back and unclasped the gold chain she wore around her neck. The church key on its end fitted the lock on the steel door.

Shoving open the door, Venice stepped inside, followed by Slater. Beyond the door there was a narrow tunnel. Its low ceiling was strung with bare electric bulbs in wire cages. The walls were made out of poured concrete. The floor was partially flooded, probably because the tunnel's path cut across the natural water table.

"The tunnel runs about a half mile due north," Venice said. "Terra Nova had it built in case he ever needed to make a fast getaway from the feds. In order to keep it secret, he had all the contractors iced."

"You sure find out a lot through pillow talk," Slater ventured with a grim smile.

"Don't put me down, Slater," she answered him in a harsh whisper as they proceeded cautiously along the dank escape tunnel. "We all have our jobs to do, each in our own different way."

"Yeah, each in our own way," Slater returned. Then he added, "Exactly what are you. DEA, maybe?"

"The DEA recruited me," she returned, "but it's more complicated than that. My husband was an agent. He was stationed in Thailand. The corruption there was incredible. The long and the short of it was that he got taken down, and I wanted to do something about it."

"So this is the way you paid your dues," Slater offered. "By working undercover. And I . . . I misunderstood."

"Well, you couldn't help it. But I had to try and get something on you because I thought you were Francisco's man. Later, I began to have my doubts about that. And yes, wanted to pay my dues. It doesn't matter who pulled the trigger or what part of the world it happened in. People like Terra Nova and Carne are all cut from the same cloth. All of them are little Hitlers shooting for the same thing—limitless power. They have to be stopped in their tracks."

Suddenly there were the sounds of slapping shoe leather and shouting voices coming from behind them. Slater didn't have to turn around to know that another hit squad was right behind them.

He and Venice rushed ahead, but seconds later the pursuers got them in range of their guns. The stuttering of automatic fire from behind them sent bullets whining at their heels as they ricocheted off the floor and walls of the escape tunnel.

Slater and Venice broke to opposite sides of the tunnel. They dropped down to reduce their target profiles as much as possible and cut loose with side-to-side volleys of whizzing parabellum steel from their auto-weapons.

The concentrated fire forced the Mexicans to tuck their heads down. In the few seconds while the answering fire was temporarily suppressed, Venice and Slater broke from their positions and ran like hell. Almost at once the firing started right up again, now coupled with the shouts and curses of their pursuers.

Slater and Venice sped ahead down the tunnel, snapping intermittent bursts of autofire over their shoulders. Minutes later they finally reached the tunnel's end.

It terminated in a rectangular pit with cinder-block walls about twenty feet deep. Overhead stretched the plank floor of a building above them. Set in that floor was a trapdoor. Running down the side of the foundation wall nearest to the tunnel entrance was a crude wooden ladder.

"The trapdoor leads to the basement of a safe house in Texas. Sometimes it's used by Terra Nova's mules," she said to Slater. "Let's hope nobody's at home."

They were about to hustle up the ladder when sudden automatic fire coming from behind them wailed out its chattering death knell. Venice clutched her temple as she crumpled, struck by a ricocheting 9 mm slug fragment the size of a nailhead that had penetrated her brain.

Slater jumped back against the wall and sprayed the pursuing death squad with the MAC, hitting some and forcing the rest to retreat back into the tunnel.

When the Ingram's clip ran dry, Slater grabbed up Venice's discarded H&K and snapped off sound-suppressed bursts at the three surviving Mexicans.

Sustaining multiple hits in vital areas, the terminated shooters dropped to the tunnel floor. Breaking from cover, Slater crouched over the wounded woman and checked her vital signs. She was fading fast. Her eyes were already starting to glaze over, and a moment later Venice shivered and then went still.

Slater's eyes took on a hard, steely glint as he climbed the ladder with Venice slung over his shoulder. He emerged into the basement of the house and cautiously picked his way up the stairs, his weapon pointed in front of him. It was a single-story house, he discovered, and well furnished. There was an operational phone and a TV.

Slater laid Venice's bloody remains on the couch. He'd see that someone came for them. He knew better than to stick around or attempt to use the phone, though. He hustled out the door just as an Audi careered up the driveway and two pony-tailed hardmen in baggy clothes jumped out of its doors, full-auto hardware bulging in their fists.

Slater ducked back around the corner of the single-story ranch house. When Terra Nova's men came rushing into the range of his gun, he jumped out on a half crouch and opened up with the MP-5. Chest-level strikes put them both away. The two enforcers went down, dropping their weapons and splattering the asphalt with blood.

Slater found the keys to the highway in the ignition. As he started up the car, one of the downed hardmen who still had some life left in him suddenly popped up from beneath the front bumper. Bleeding profusely, he threw his arms across the hood and tried to climb on top of it.

Slater thought about what Terra Nova's scum had done to Venice as he floored the gas pedal and rammed the car straight into the buttonman. Catapulted forward by the terrific force of impact, his head crashed into the windshield, spattering it with a shower of blood before his mangled corpse rolled off and hit the blacktop.

Slater punched the windshield-wiper button and he saw jets of soapy fluid cut twin vertical streaks across the bloody glaze. Cranking up the wipers, he accelerated the Audi flat out onto the freeway.

28

Francisco Terra Nova sipped vodka chilled to the point where it had begun to thicken and watched the two naked, moaning women writhe on the luminous screen in the stateroom of his yacht.

They were skilled at what they were doing, and Terra Nova enjoyed their performance while he sipped the iced vodka and repeatedly brought the platinum coke spoon to his left nostril. He didn't feel that he wanted any live bodies around him just then, and this gave him the diversion he needed.

He had been a little nervous since he'd hurriedly left Mexico days before, but now he was feeling somewhat better.

Despite the millions in payoff money in the hands of American and Mexican officials, his luck hadn't been running true to form lately.

Since he had met a guy named Deal Slater, to be precise. The moment that Slater had come into the picture, everything had turned sour. He had been stupid, yes. But self-recrimination wouldn't help him now, he realized.

Slater was history, and Terra Nova knew that he himself belonged to the future.

The *Choc Mool* had been sailing on a southeasterly course across the gulf and Terra Nova had been half expecting to be challenged and hove to by a U.S. Coast Guard cutter. It hadn't happened, though. That had only been his paranoia talking.

The one-hundred-fifteen-foot power yacht had emerged into the Caribbean waters completely unhampered. Only then had Terra Nova felt that he could breathe easily. These crystalline waters were far less hazardous to traffickers than those directly bordering American shores.

Here he could sit out his exile from Mexico in comfort and style until the heat died down. And he had no doubt whatever that the heat was turned on big-time. Slater was no mere merc, Terra Nova had finally learned through his secret sources, confirming his late-dawning suspicions.

Slater *was* the heat. Slater *was* big-time.

Slater was The Man.

Terra Nova had begun collecting pieces of who and what Slater actually was, and soon he would have the puzzle completely assembled. He'd been suckered, yes, scammed, yes, but stopped cold—no way, no day. The Mexican was bigger than even Slater was and would make sure that the blow dealt him was roundly avenged.

With a line up his nose, Terra Nova finally reached a violent sexual climax as the perfectly sculpted bodies of the two women shivered feverishly and they cried out in the final throes of mutual pleasure.

What Terra Nova needed now was a dip in the yacht's pool to cap a singularly rewarding experience. Standing on the diving board, he plunged into the ice-cold waters, savoring the shock to his already tingling flesh. Bobbing to the surface moments later, he felt like a man reborn.

PORTING M-16s and wearing camouflage fatigues, the contingent of Mexican feds stormed the gate of Terra Nova's fortress mansion on the Guadalajara heights. Deal Slater went inside the compound along with the pointmen of the raid.

Beyond its high stone walls, the druglord's citadel was deserted, except for a skeleton crew of servants and ground keepers who checked out clean and knew nothing—or claimed to know nothing—about the present whereabouts of their missing employer.

With Terra Nova and his crew of buttonmen absent from the scene, the feds declared that there was nothing more they could do except keep U.S. DEA officials posted in the event that Terra Nova should reappear. This, of course, meant that the feds had let the druglord go scot-free in the first place.

The raid on the Octagon was only a piece of hurried face-saving by embarrassed Mexican officials. Behind the hollow and none too convincing charade was the reality that Terra Nova's cronies high up in the Mexican government had no intention of allowing U.S. authorities to legally extradite him.

Hours later Slater was back across the border in Laredo, Texas, where Hawke and Bishop had set up a command post in a hotel room. They hadn't been idle while their boss was interfacing with the Mexican feds. The two SLAM commandos had been monitoring late-breaking Intelligence concerning the drug baron's current situation.

His two partners informed Slater that Terra Nova's yacht had been located in Caribbean waters and conclusively identified by Coast Guard air-sea surveillance assets. The locals had been informed that Terra Nova was wanted for questioning, but not unexpectedly, they were dragging their feet in apprehending him.

Terra Nova's dirty money went a long way down in that part of the world—as it did most everywhere else.

What this meant was that SLAM had only one response left open now. It was the response that they'd been using effectively all along, however.

The force option.

29

The CAT 900 shallow-draft, ultrafast assault-and-interceptor craft knifed through the sparkling blue waters like a swift sea predator closing for the kill.

A Vulcan 20 mm cannon was bolted atop the roof of the CAT's cabin. Aft of the needle-nosed prow a .50-caliber machine gun was gimbal mounted for a 180-degree field of fire capability.

The CAT could achieve speeds of up to eighty knots. Its sleek hull configuration made it highly maneuverable as it skimmed the ocean surface.

At the controls of the CAT sat Deal Slater. Behind him, his gloved hands clutching the spade grips of the Vulcan gun, Mason Hawke stood at the ready. Seated in the forward machine-gunner's well of the sleek prow of the shark-nosed attack cruiser was Eddie Bishop, his hands curled around the stock and trigger of the box-fed .50-caliber gun.

Long-range radar had confirmed the *Choc Mool*'s position dead ahead. Before very long they had gotten their first unaided visual confirmation of the craft's position.

They could see the sleek one-hundred-fifteen-footer lying about five hundred yards to port, anchored in the placid, crystal blue waters of the Caribbean, its white hull drenched by the tropical sun.

Waiting for the kill.

THE WOMAN'S FINGERS moved skillfully across Terra Nova's bare, suntanned back, massaging stiff muscles, kneading hidden pressure points. She was Japanese and skilled in the ancient art of shiatsu massage, as well as other, more erotic Oriental specialties.

Every muscle in his body had become completely relaxed when sudden commotion from the aft deck reached his ears.

"*Jefe,* there is trouble coming!" one of his enforcers advised him, rushing over to where he lay beneath the hot sun on the foredeck of the yacht.

Terra Nova rose so rapidly that he knocked the woman off his back and sent her toppling onto her rump. He was instantly conscious of the type of trouble he was most likely in for.

The deep and abiding calm that he had felt earlier had been deceptive. Just beneath the surface was the nagging suspicion that precisely what was happening now would eventually take place.

Terra Nova had known in his gut that Slater wouldn't quit. The man operated beyond the law and didn't give a damn about jurisdictional niceties.

Terra Nova had become weakened by years of dealing with corrupt men whose loyalty and cooperation could be assured with money and bolstered with threats. Here he was dealing with a new breed of antagonist: a man who, unlike others, didn't care about either incentive.

The druglord ripped the high-powered Zeiss-Nikon binoculars from the enforcer's hands. Raising them to his eyes, he scanned the blue-green seas until he picked out the profile of the sleek assault craft and the three commandos who manned it.

The interceptor craft was now close enough for Terra Nova to recognize the features of the pilot in the wheelhouse.

Slater. Of course.

"Total that boat!" Terra Nova shouted at his waiting hatchet man. "Quickly! Blow it right out of the water!"

"Yes, *jefe!* It is as good as done, *jefe!*"

The Mexican gunman turned and began shouting orders to the rest of the crew who stood watching from the deck below.

The armed crew of mercenary soldiers had been retained in the event of just this contingency. Terra Nova hadn't left Mexico without first preparing a small yet capable commando assault team to act as his bodyguard for the duration of his exile from home base.

In minutes three Zodiacs carrying Terra Nova's mercs were roaring away from the mother ship at high speed. The blacksuited, grim-faced men on board the light assault craft carried weapons that were locked and loaded as they closed on the intercepting CAT.

"LOOKS LIKE we've got company," Slater sang out.

With the Zodiacs interposed between the CAT and the *Choc Mool*, Slater swung the fast cruiser away from its course and began taking evasive action. The CAT was proceeding broadside of the Zodiacs now and presented too easy a target on its present heading.

As the CAT slewed hard to port, the placid blue sea suddenly exploded into geysers of white spray around its flanks.

The two 40 mm mortar rounds fired from M-203 shoulder launchers had scored near-misses, and Slater's fast thinking had just avoided what would otherwise have been a disastrous collision.

Before the Zodiac shooters had a chance to launch another mortar salvo, Hawke and Bishop got cracking with their own automatic firepower.

The Vulcan gun's barrels were swiveled into position, and clouds of gray-brown smoke marked the ejection of scores of hard-core 20 mm rounds. Meanwhile, the machine gun at the prow of the CAT chattered away, hurling glowing tracer rounds toward the trio of Zodiacs.

A flying wedge of fast-rotoring steel caught the M-203 gunner in the lead Zodiac high on his chest just as he was pulling the trigger of the shoulder-fired grenade launcher.

The two wings of the wedge tore apart his heart and lungs. The inner point ripped away most of his head, spraying blood and brain tissue across the Zodiac.

As his lifeless body pitched sideways, the 40 mm grenade can he was about to fire shot straight into the face of the pilot sitting at the stern. The pilot's head was blown off in a burst of blood, then the entire craft exploded.

The burning Zodiac soon collapsed in the choppy sea. The other two pursuit craft broke formation and veered to the left and right of the sinking inflatable, spewing out automatic fire targeted on the sea-skimming CAT.

Slater's piloting skill kept the CAT out of the blitzing automatic fire as Hawke and Bishop launched their superior firepower from prow and stern.

The outcome of the battle was predictable from the start. Sustaining hit after hit from both the Vulcan and the .50-caliber machine gun, the two remaining Zodiacs exploded into gigantic balloons of fire that ascended toward the sky. Acrid smoke from burning rubber rose from the two funeral pyres floating on the ocean. The merc survivor count was zero.

The CAT veered hard around, throwing up sprays of foam, its knife-edged prow bouncing off the surface chop as it sped past the flaming wreckage to vector in for the final takedown on the *Choc Mool* herself.

30

The captain of the *Choc Mool* opened the throttles wide. The powerful diesel turbines propelled the yacht through the waters at a speed of close to fifty knots.

Despite the yacht's high speed, Slater easily closed the gap between the CAT and the rapidly moving vessel.

With the Zodiacs and their crews of gunmen out of commission, catching up with the escaping pleasure craft was a foregone conclusion.

More black-garbed gunmen had appeared on port and starboard gunwales of the sleek white yacht. They immediately opened up on the fast-closing interceptor with automatic small-arms weapons.

Hawke and Bishop sighted on the brace of gunmen who were silhouetted against the blue sky while Slater maintained the CAT at the maximum-range limits of their weapons.

The superior reach and firepower of the Vulcan and the Browning took care of the rest. The small-arms fire hammering down from the *Choc Mool* just couldn't hope to match the heavy-duty armament packed by the CAT.

A single combined burst from the heavy guns deployed on the CAT sent the hardmen who were firing from the yacht tumbling into the sea, their bodies punctured with bullet wounds.

Slater swung the CAT hard around, and Hawke and Bishop resighted their weapons on the second tier of mercs whom Terra Nova had set up. They were quickly knocked down by the three SLAM commandos' superior aim and firing power.

A few minutes of trading fire, and the mercs stationed on the port bow of the yacht had also been cut down. There were no more gunmen lined up to trade fire with the pursuers.

Slater now drew the sleek prow of the CAT abreast of the yacht's stern as Hawke and Bishop unshipped grapnel-firing armament. A pull on the trigger sent grappling hooks with mil-spec ropes in tow snaking across the open water between the CAT and the *Choc Mool*.

The hooked grapnels gaffed on the yacht's steel railing. Slater throttled down and then cut power altogether after Hawke and Bishop made the ropes fast to cleats bolted to the CAT's hull.

The *Choc Mool* would now tow the CAT along behind it as it sped on its course.

While Hawke and Bishop continued to man their weapon stations, Slater hefted his own grapnel gun and fired a knotted climbing rope over the *Choc Mool*'s bow. He scaled the stern of the yacht and hauled himself over the gunwale railing.

The bodies of gunmen littered the deck in bloody disarray. Slater scanned the yacht's aft area, his Commando SMG sweeping in short arcs, ready for sudden attack. But there was no sign of movement on board.

No sign of Terra Nova.

Slater dogtrotted toward the vessel's prow. Suddenly he spotted fleeting movement behind one of the giant steel funnels rising up from the deck.

Slater sprinted across open deck space to take cover behind a bulkhead a few feet from the funnel. Breaking from concealment after a three-count, he dashed laterally toward the funnel, then quickly wheeled around to point his SMG at whoever was hiding there. Slater looked down the sights of his Colt Commando at the cowering Japanese woman.

Her large doe eyes were wide and pleading, her full breasts bare. Not expecting to have found what he had, Slater dropped his guard for a split second. Behind him, on the bridge above, Terra Nova popped from cover suddenly and leveled a Beretta M3P bullpup combat shotgun at the SLAM commando standing on the deck below.

But Slater had caught the flash of movement from the bridge reflected in a wet slick on the deck. Combat reflexes took control, and he ducked sideways just as a spreading fan of buckshot demolished the five-foot-square section of deck where he'd been standing moments earlier.

The shotgun's report was still echoing in the stiff sea wind when Slater darted across the foredeck to take cover beneath the bridge as more fire from up top came hammering down at him.

Slater counted ten beats, then leaped from cover and launched a suppressing burst of slugs upward where he figured they'd find Terra Nova.

But the druglord was already gone, and the lethal burst passed harmlessly through empty air.

Slater hustled up the metal stairs leading to the bridge and found it completely deserted, except for one very dead body in the wheelhouse. The body belonged to the skipper of the *Choc Mool*, who sagged lifelessly in his pilot's chair.

The bloody hole in the side of his head offered grim testament to the price he'd paid, probably for contradicting an order Terra Nova had given him. Set on autopilot, the vessel was now proceeding on a preprogrammed course heading.

Almost certainly the skipper, citing the presence of treacherous coral reefs in the region, had insisted on heaving to. Just as certainly Terra Nova had demanded otherwise, and sealed the captain's fate.

Slater dodged back down the stairs to search for Terra Nova below decks. The doors to cabin after cabin opened from the main companionway, each of them harboring potential danger.

The *Choc Mool* was a large, spacious craft and she had been specially built to carry many passengers on long oceangoing junkets.

Reluctantly Slater was forced to conduct a door-to-door search in the confines of the narrow companionway. Slow and hazardous, the process ate up precious time but was the only way to winnow down the number of places his quarry had left to hide in. He moved along grimly, not knowing what would greet him each time he crouched in a doorway, his gun probing the interior. He only had three more doors to go.

Breathing raggedly, the bullpup in his hands, Terra Nova had his back to the wall beside the cabin door.

He could hear Slater outside, opening and closing doors, and he knew that the next one he'd come to would be his own. There was no place else to hide, though, and nothing else left to do except to gamble everything on a single roll of the dice.

Terra Nova took a deep breath, then flung open the second-last door and jumped out into the companionway, the bullpup low on his hip. His gamble had paid off.

The unexpected move had caught Slater by complete surprise, and Terra Nova now stood leveling the bullpup at Slater's gut region.

The sudden smile that lit up his angular face spoke volumes about the triumph that the druglord felt coursing through him in an almost orgasmic rush.

The smile said "you lose."

The blast sounded like thunder in the narrow confines of the cramped companionway. But instead of Slater, it was Terra Nova who sagged against the wall, the lopsided smile still plastered on his aquiline face. Heavy-caliber rounds fired in rapid succession had ripped into him, leaving behind ragged holes.

Behind him, looking scared witless, was the half-clad Japanese woman. Slater reached forward and took the smoking Desert Eagle Magnum pistol from her quaking hands. She fell forward into his arms, sobbing on his shoulder, and Slater could feel her fear-erected nipples pressing against him.

"Come on," he yelled at her, yanking off his shirt and covering her nakedness.

They had to make tracks immediately.

The yacht had no pilot. The *Choc Mool* was now hopelessly out of control, loose-cannoning around the

Caribbean and overdue for a fatal collision with the coral reefs that infested the area.

Slater and the woman emerged from the maze of staterooms below decks, and Slater quickly saw to his chagrin that the yacht was seconds away from crashing headlong into a coral atoll that had loomed up only a few hundred yards off the starboard bow.

Racing toward the stern of the yacht with the stunned woman in tow, Slater eyeballed the CAT a dozen or so yards behind the *Choc Mool*. The grapnel lines fired earlier had now been severed by Hawke and Bishop as a safety precaution, and the CAT was holding steady with the yacht's course under her own power.

Slater could now see Hawke and Bishop waving at him from the CAT and saw also that their lips were moving frantically. He couldn't hear what they were saying at that distance but he would have been surprised if it wasn't "jump!"

That was precisely what Slater did, throwing a life preserver around the girl and pushing his terrified charge into the sea a split second ahead of him.

Both hit the water at approximately the same time, buffeted by the turbulence of the *Choc Mool*'s prop wash.

Slater grabbed the floundering woman and propelled her toward the CAT in a rescue carry as he swam

Omega Force is caught dead center in a brutal Middle East war in the next episode of

OMEGA

by PATRICK F. ROGERS

In Book 2: **ZERO HOUR**, the Omega Force is dispatched on a search-and-destroy mission to eliminate enemies of the U.S. seeking revenge for Iraq's defeat in the Gulf—enemies who will use any means necessary to trigger a full-scale war.

With capabilities unmatched by any other paramilitary organization in the world, Omega Force is a special ready-reaction antiterrorist strike force composed of the best commandos and equipment the military has to offer.

**A new age of terrorism
calls for a new breed of hero**

NOMAD

S M A R T   B O M B

D A V I D   A L E X A N D E R

**Code name: Nomad. He is the supreme fighting
machine, a new breed of elite commando
whose specialty is battling 21st-century
techno-terrorism with bare-knuckle combat
skills and state-of-the-art weapons.**

**Desperately racing against a lethal countdown,
Nomad tracks a rogue weapons expert but runs
into a trap. He comes face-to-face with his
hated nemesis in a deadly contest—a contest in
which the odds are stacked against him.**

WELCOME TO

JAMES AXLER

DEATH LANDS.
Shockscape

**A shockscape with a view—
and the danger is free.**

Ryan and his band of warrior survivalists chart a perilous journey
across the desolate Rocky Mountains. Their mission: Deliver the hired
killers of a small boy to his avenging father.

In the Deathlands, survival is a gamble. Death is the only sure bet.

THE FREEDOM TRILOGY

Join Mack Bolan's fight for freedom in the freedom trilogy...

Beginning in June 1993, Gold Eagle presents a special three-book in-line continuity featuring Mack Bolan, the Executioner, along with ABLE TEAM and PHOENIX FORCE, as they face off against a communist dictator. A dictator with far-reaching plans to gain control of the troubled Baltic state area and whose ultimate goal is world supremacy. The fight for freedom starts in June with **THE EXECUTIONER #174: Battle Plan**, continues in **THE EXECUTIONER #175: Battle Ground**, and concludes in August with the longer 352-page Mack Bolan novel **Battle Force.**

Available at your favorite retail outlets in
June through to August.

GOLD
EAGLE ®

FT93-1